THE GOODBYES

By Leslie Welch

BlueMoon PUBLISHERS

ADVANCE PRAISE FOR *THE GOODBYES*

"I got motion sickness on the metro because I couldn't stop reading *The Goodbyes* by Leslie Welch."
- Deborah Siegel, Author, *The Popularity Plan*

"*The Goodbyes* captures the fragility, anger, and sexual exploration of a modern American adolescence. Webb Turner is a complex character grappling with coming of age in an era when talent and fame can minimize the deeper journey toward adulthood. It's an exciting story that showcases how music can not only pull us back into memories, but also propel us forward into new moments full of hope."
- Laura Berry, Owner and CEO, Cogberry Creative

"Leslie Welch has a knack for making you feel. You love her characters, you sympathize with them, and sometimes you just want to knock some sense into them. *The Goodbyes* takes you for an emotional ride down the road to adulthood. For anyone who has ever pined, I highly recommend *The Goodbyes*."
- Camille Zions, Goodreads Reviewer

"I enjoyed this story of a young man with remarkable gifts."
- Margaret Holmes, Goodreads reviewer

"Really enjoyed reading this book. Could not put it down until I was done at 1am! It was frustrating, funny, and sad. 5/5"
- Allison Kelley, Goodreads reviewer

COPYRIGHT INFORMATION

CONTENTS

To Adam, for encouraging me to "Finish the damn book,"
reading my crappy first drafts, and answering my weird questions
(even at four a.m.).

To Jules, for being a much cooler person at thirteen than I could
ever hope to be.

To Mere, for living in imaginary worlds with me (despite the fact
that I'd never let you be the heroine).

To my mom, for giving me a life full of experiences.

CHAPTER ONE · WWDC STUDIO, ROCKVILLE, MARYLAND

January 22, 2016

A few shots of tequila usually took care of the anxiety, but it had been three months since Webb had a drink. He was on his own, feeling naked, forgetful, and unprepared. He could write thousands of perfect words that captured his thoughts, but when he tried to say them out loud, he became an observer, detached from his mouth—helpless to stop the rambling words and long pauses.

On the ride from New York to D.C., Charlotte had given up her only chance to sleep to help him prepare for the interview. But as the intern led them through the radio station, Webb could feel the memorized responses breaking down into static.

"I wasn't supposed to work today. I paid someone to switch," the intern said, holding open the studio door. "I'm a big fan."

"Thanks, man. That means a lot," Webb said.

"Would you mind?" the intern asked, holding out a CD and a Sharpie.

"I didn't know anyone bought these anymore," Webb said, taking the disc. "What's your name?"

"Connor."

Webb scribbled *Connor, Thanks for everything, Webb Turner* next to the list of songs on the back.

Webb adjusted the headphones and settled in front of the microphone. Connor placed a bottle of water in front of him. "Is chilled water ok?"

Webb nodded and gave the kid a smile. Unlike Brent, Webb didn't care about the temperature of his water.

Dozens of stickers with the station's call sign obscured the view out of the fifth-floor window. The sky blazed red and orange. Webb snapped a picture and posted it to Instagram. He'd seen almost every sunrise for the last two months, but none of them had bled with this brilliance.

"What's that saying? Red in the morning, sailors take warning?" the DJ asked from across the table.

Webb tried to remember her name. Something with a "K." Kat? He met so many people on the road, they all morphed together; human shapes with minor variations of hair, skin, and height. She fit into the alt-rock pixie variety. Her black hair pointed away from her head in a disorderly halo, almost the same as his.

"That sounds right. My grandma used to say that," Webb said.

"Mine too." She smiled. "Are you ready?"

"I guess so," Webb said.

She slid the faders up and leaned in to her microphone.

"D.C. 101. That was 'Lonely Boy' by The Black Keys, and you're waking up with me, Cate Donnelly. We have a special treat for you this morning. You may know him as the guitarist and songwriter for one of today's most successful bands, or if you're a reality TV buff, you'll know him as the 'nice' mentor on *Songwrite*. I'd like to welcome Webb Turner of TempFive to the studio."

"Thanks, Cate. It's great to be here," he lied. He could feel his pulse in his neck, threatening to cut off his breath.

"It's been another big year for the band. You have a sold-out show tonight at the Verizon Center. You just played two sold-out shows at Madison Square Garden. How are you holding up?"

"I'm tired." Webb laughed. "But I can't complain."

"I guess it's a little early for you."

"Actually, it's late. I haven't been to bed yet," he said, forcing a smile. He should've been crawling into his bunk on the tour bus now, waiting for Ambien to drag him into sleep.

"Well, thanks for staying up for us," she cooed. "Are you looking forward to anything when the tour is over?"

"That's a good question. I've never had a break this long. Usually, we'd go back to the studio to record another album, or I'd work on *Songwrite*. I guess I'm looking forward to going home for a while to see my family." He relaxed his hands, relieved that the words hadn't left him.

"You grew up in Pennsylvania, right?"

"Yes, Glen Hope."

"Never heard of it before today."

"It's really hard to see on a map. You really have to zoom in," Webb joked. "I usually just tell people that I grew up near Penn State."

"Have they named a street after you or anything?"

"There aren't that many streets to rename, but I wouldn't be surprised if my grandma put a 'Home of Webb Turner' plaque on my mom's house."

"Your mom must be proud of you."

Charlotte flashed her acknowledgement across the room to Webb. Until a few months ago, it had been years since he'd spoken with his mom.

"I... I don't know. I hope so," he said, wiping his hands on his thighs.

Cate leaned in. "You know, I find it interesting that anyone who's ever worked with you says you're a nice guy. I also heard you live in a studio apartment. Would you say that you're not a typical celebrity?"

"I'm not sure how to answer that. Technically, I have a studio apartment on each coast." He chuckled. "But I try to remember that besides my job, I'm not different from anyone. I'm a simple guy who has a very visible career."

"You put your pants on one leg at a time..."

"Not exactly. I have a staff of two who dress me, but other than that, I'm completely normal." Cate played along with his joke, offering to dress him if someone called in sick. He relaxed. Why was he so worried? Just as he started to think about giving more interviews, the conversation shifted.

"You recently started The Hope Foundation. Can you tell us a little about it?"

Charlotte stopped typing and looked up. That question wasn't on the list.

"Well, um, it's a foundation for people—I mean patients who are waiting for organ transplants. We have money, I mean grants, to cover medical expenses, housing, stuff like that." His thoughts unravelled. He didn't know how to talk about the foundation.

"The first grant recipient, Bree Brewer, is from your hometown, isn't she?" Cate asked. Her voice remained friendly, but her eyes narrowed.

The room grew smaller as Webb's panic ballooned. Bree. Hearing this stranger say her name tore a gash in the composure he was trying so hard to maintain. He could swear that the walls were inflating.

"Yeah. She is. I knew her growing up."

Charlotte jumped up and motioned for Cate to cut the feed.

"We'll hear more from Webb after the break," Cate said. She pulled the faders back down.

"What the fuck are you doing?" Charlotte said as soon as the "On Air" light faded. "We didn't approve these questions."

"I didn't mean to—"

"Yes, you did," Charlotte snapped.

"I thought it was interesting. Usually people like to talk about their charity work," Cate said with feigned innocence.

"We're here to promote the tour, not satisfy your dreams of being an investigative journalist. If you can't—"

"It's ok, Char," Webb interrupted. "It just caught me off guard. I'll finish the interview, but I don't want to talk about the foundation."

"No problem," Cate said. "We'll just talk about the weather."

CHAPTER TWO - VERIZON CENTER, WASHINGTON, D.C.

January 22, 2016

Webb woke alone on the tour bus outside Verizon Center, shivering and still groggy from the sleeping pills. Brent, Chris, and Garrett were indulging at a chef's table somewhere in Penn Quarter. They didn't invite him. He wouldn't have gone even if they did. He only spent money when he had to.

When he came back from the interview, Webb had told the driver to keep the engine off. He almost regretted it now that most of the heat had seeped out of the parked bus. But part of him needed the reminder. The icy air. The feeling that he'd never be warm. It reminded him of home.

He contemplated wandering into the stadium, but he couldn't peel himself from the coffin-like bunk to find Charlotte. She'd be too busy to talk anyway. He drifted back into the dark, prescription sleep to stay warm.

HIS PHONE vibrated in the cubby above his head until it went to voicemail. A few seconds later, it rumbled again. He felt around for it, afraid he'd lost track of time and was late for soundcheck. No, soundcheck was over; he might be late for the show. He'd waited too long to take the Ambien.

He tore through the energy bar wrappers and water bottles until he found his phone. Two missed calls from Charlotte and a voicemail from his mom. He stared at the message, hesitating before he played it. There were two things he never did before a show: eat and check his messages. He only heard the first few words before the roar of panic blocked out the sound of his mom's voice.

Webb tore back the heavy curtain and stumbled out into the narrow hall. He pulled his suitcase down from the "junk bunk" above his bed, threw his phone inside, zipped it up, and placed it on his mattress.

AS SOON as he found Charlotte, she pushed a dry-cleaned jacket at him. They were all wearing matching costumes now. Brent's idea.

"Where've you been? You're going on—like, now." She pressed the side of her earpiece. "He's here. Getting him into wardrobe."

"I can't," he said.

"I know it's stupid, but you have to wear it," Charlotte said. He knew the fatigue in her tone wasn't directed at him. The bluish crescents under her eyes looked darker than they had this morning. She still hadn't slept. He hesitated before he gave her one more thing to worry about. She shook out a handful of peanut M&Ms and picked out a blue one. "Here's a good luck charm," she said, handing it to him. He clutched it in his palm.

"I can't play tonight. I have to go. Bree…" He stopped himself from saying it out loud.

"I know she's sick, but you have to wait until after the tour." She pressed the button again. "I said he's on his fucking way."

"She's dying, Char. My mom said they don't think she'll make it through the night."

He watched her expression change from "Take No Shit Manager Charlotte" to "Best Friend Char."

"Oh, God, Webb. I'm sorry." She pressed her fist to her mouth and bit the knuckle of her thumb, like she did when she was solving his problems.

The pain crested, working its way from his chest to his eyes. "I can't do this." He wanted to let go and fold into a heap of anguish on the floor.

"Yes, you can. Get out there, play your ass off, and I'll work on getting you home right after the show, ok?"

He nodded and popped the M&M into his mouth.

"Now, put this stupid jacket on."

Webb shrugged into the military-style jacket, shifted his eyes down, and ran through the darkened hall. A small army of stagehands ushered him into place behind Brent and Chris.

"You ok?" Chris asked. Webb shook his head.

They burst into a storm of applause and flashes. His automatic steps fell in the wrong direction—away from the girl who had captured him in her gravity thirteen years ago.

CHAPTER THREE - GLEN HOPE, PENNSYLVANIA

August 10, 2002

Webb was out the door and buckled into the front seat before his mom could grab her purse. He'd do anything to shorten the trip to the mall. He had to finish the fort in the woods with Jason. They had spent most of the summer scavenging their sheds and hauling building scraps to a spot next to the stream. It was almost done.

"Get in the back. The new people don't know where the mall is, so I offered to take them," his mom said.

"What? Mom!" he objected, but it was too late. The new lady was already crossing the street with her yellow-and-purple-haired daughter in tow.

The girl focused on her feet as she shuffled across the road, so Webb only saw the top of her head. The stripes in her hair looked like she had painted them on with finger paints.

He groaned and climbed into the back. When the door opened, and the girl stepped inside, Webb looked into her eyes and froze. He hoped the terror growing inside him wasn't showing. He was breathing wrong, he could tell.

She tossed a quick glance his way. He wondered if she could see every nerve sparking in his body. He imagined his skin growing transparent, showing his blood pumping, his breakfast digesting, his brain thinking weird thoughts.

"Bree's starting seventh grade, too," his mom said.

He didn't trust his voice, so he nodded.

As they pulled out of the driveway, Webb wasn't upset that he'd be stuck in the car for almost an hour. Nothing could be more excruciating and interesting than sitting next to her.

Webb stared at the lines of her profile. Her rounded nose. Her lips, puffy and thick in the middle. The shade reminded him of cherry Fun Dip.

She snapped her head and looked at him. "Why do you keep staring at me? Haven't you ever seen a girl before?"

Webb floundered for words. "Your hair. It's cool."

Was looking at a girl supposed to physically hurt?

"Oh, thanks," she said, smoothing her hair with her palm. Brittle chunks of paint crumbled into her hand. She clutched the purple flecks in her fist as she turned back to the window.

WHEN THEY got to the mall, Webb was in such a daze, he didn't protest when his mom made him try on three different sizes of khaki pants.

"You're growing so fast. I think we should buy a larger size…"

His mom explained how she could make them fit until he grew into them, but Webb hardly heard her. He couldn't stop replaying Bree saying, "Oh, thanks," in his head. He didn't want to look at anything except the sun streaming through the car window, igniting the palette of white, yellow, and purple. He had to talk to her, to say something that didn't sound stupid, something that would entice her to exchange more sentences, words—anything.

He agreed to almost every piece of clothing his mom suggested: the fake polo shirts, the no-name shoes that made his feet smell like cheap glue and poverty. It all seemed unimportant. The only thing he could focus on was getting to the food court.

HIS MOM got in line at Sbarro.

"Do you want pepperoni or sausage?" she asked.

Pizza didn't seem sophisticated enough.

"Can I get Chinese?" he asked.

"You always get pizza," his mom argued.

"I think I should try something new..."

She handed him a ten-dollar bill and asked for change. He didn't know what he would get, but whatever it was, he hoped it would impress Bree.

Webb stared at the steaming metal tubs of bite-sized meats and vegetables. He pointed to the least offensive-looking meat, puffy with batter and fried to a pale, yellowish brown.

On the way to the table, he fought the regret that he didn't get pizza—especially when he saw a giant slice in front of Bree.

"Did you get some nice clothes?" Mrs. Brewer asked as Webb settled into the empty seat across from Bree.

He nodded, watching Bree fold the piece of pepperoni pizza in half. Before she took a bite, she caught the clear, red grease in her mouth.

Here he had a direct view of her. It was easier to see every subtle movement she made. He could memorize her, like the Pledge of Allegiance.

"I like what you did to your hair," his mom said to Bree. "I used to dye my hair with Kool-Aid when I was your age."

"Really?" she asked, suddenly excited.

Mrs. Brewer frowned at Webb's mom and shook her head.

"Well, maybe a little older, but I always liked styling hair, and now I get paid for it."

"Is it fun?"

"I think so. And it looks like you have a special talent for it."

"How do you dye hair with Kool-Aid?" she asked.

"I can show you. It's easy," Webb's mom said.

Bree's eyes lit, but the spark quickly faded when her mom said, "I thought you wanted to be a veterinarian."

"I can do both," Bree said.

"That's ridiculous," Mrs. Brewer huffed.

"Well, if you want to learn anything about hair or makeup, our door is always open," Webb's mom said.

Bree gave her a grateful smile. Webb recorded it and hoped Bree would take his mom up on her offer.

JASON WAS waiting on Webb's porch when they got home. He saw the whole goodbye exchange with the new girl. He witnessed Webb's mom invite them all over for dinner and Mrs. Brewer not commit to a day.

When they were finally alone on the porch, Jason stared at Webb, waiting for an explanation, but Webb couldn't speak. He was too busy remembering every nuance of the afternoon, letting the changes inside him take hold. Whatever was happening terrified him, but he didn't want it to stop.

"What were you doing with the new people?" Jason finally asked.

"My mom drove them to the mall." Webb wanted to say more, to talk about her, but he didn't want to introduce Jason to the secret that Bree wasn't just a new girl who moved to town—she was the most intriguing person he'd ever met.

"I heard her dad only has one arm, and his face melted off," Jason said.

"Where'd you hear that?"

"My mom." Jason changed the subject. "I found a bunch of awesome stuff for the fort." He nodded to his backpack. Webb started to unzip it.

"Not here! There's sensitive shit in there. We can open it when we get there."

They crossed the bridge, ducked through the break in the rusted fence, and followed the deer path until they reached the clearing next to the stream.

The fort sat undisturbed under the tarp that Jason had snuck out of his garage earlier in the summer. They crouched inside. Jason opened the backpack and pulled out two beers, a few cigarette butts, and two issues of *Penthouse*.

CHAPTER FOUR - GLEN HOPE, PENNSYLVANIA

March 16, 2007

Webb rushed outside to the bus stop, hoping to catch Bree before Jason came. Junior Prom was in a few weeks. He had finally worked up the courage to ask her.

He planned to ask her quickly, but making the words come out was more like pulling off a bandage that had been anchored to hairs for too long. Tense, unsure.

"Do you think you might want to... to hang out... at prom?"

Her nostrils flared, and a sympathetic smile spread across her face as soon as she realized what he was fumbling to say.

"I'm already going with Jason." She looked away.

It would have hurt less if Jason had taken an old hunting knife and stabbed him in the stomach. Webb never should have told him or even admitted that he liked someone.

He wanted to curl his hand into a furious ball and blast it across Jason's face, but he knew it would be stupid. Jason could easily flick Webb's punch away now.

"That's cool. I thought, you know, if you didn't already have a date..."

Why was he still talking?

"But we could hang out sometime," she offered.

He froze. Could she tell he couldn't move? Couldn't breathe?

"Yeah, anytime. You know where to find me…"

Oh, God, shut up, Webb.

"Are you going to Merilee Davis' St. Patrick's Day party tomorrow night? We could go together."

He wasn't going. In fact, he couldn't stand Merilee.

"I'm not invited."

She rolled her eyes playfully. "I'm inviting you."

Webb pretended to consider it for a moment. "Ok. Yeah, sure," he said with a shrug.

The truth was, he'd go anywhere she asked.

CHAPTER FIVE - GLEN HOPE, PENNSYLVANIA

March 17, 2007

 "**M**om! Do I have anything green to wear?" he yelled down the stairs. His whole wardrobe had been turning black lately.

"I have a green sweater you could borrow."

"Never mind," he called back to her. He'd just have to wear black.

Webb met Bree at her house so they could walk to the party together. She was head-to-toe in green but made it look cool. Mrs. Brewer watched them from the end of the driveway. Merilee lived half a mile away. If he walked slowly, that could translate into twenty minutes alone with Bree.

"Walk facing traffic so you can see the cars coming," Mrs. Brewer called out as they walked away.

"It must be nice not to have your mom up your ass all the time," Bree said when they had escaped her mom's earshot. "We should get on a bus and never come back."

"Where would we go?" He played along, happy to be included in her fantasy.

"I don't know. California? I could be an actress. You could be a professional surfer."

"I don't know how to swim," he said.

"I'll teach you."

"I really don't want to be a surfer."

"Why? Are you afraid of sharks?" she teased.

"No."

"Fine. You can be a rock star then."

"That's better."

He imagined the California sun burning away his inevitable life of working the third shift, melting his future into hers.

"You know what's weird? We live across the street from each other, but we've never hung out," she said.

"That's not true. We went to the mall together when you moved here."

"I forgot about that!"

"You had purple streaks in your hair."

"I was so weird." She flipped her hair to the other side. The apple-scented breeze intoxicated Webb before it evaporated around him. "I did it to get back at my mom for making me move here," she said.

"Yeah, we all thought that was pretty weird. Not your hair—I mean, no one moves here. I thought your hair was cool."

"I thought you were cool with your sweet-and-sour chicken. My dad hates Chinese food, so we never order it." She kicked a large stone.

They fell into silence, shuffling down the road. He pictured her dad with one arm and a melted face and winced.

"Jason told me that you guys built a pretty epic fort," she said as they passed the Sunoco.

Webb smiled, letting his pride show a little. It had turned out to be an epic fort. "I haven't been back there since seventh grade."

"Do you think it's still there?"

"Probably…"

She turned to him, eyes large with excitement. "We should go see if it is."

"It's on the way," he said, encouraged by the prospect of more alone time with her. He hoped the two-room shack wasn't better in his memories—if it was still standing at all.

Webb led her to the break in the fence, and they hiked in the direction of the fort. The deer path was overgrown but still visible. Even though he'd walked there a hundred times, he felt like he might get lost or make a fool of himself. But the idea of seclusion, just the two of them, spurred him forward.

She reached for his hand. The contact of her skin caught Webb off guard. He stumbled over a rock but quickly caught himself.

When he heard the stream, he let his breath escape and made an effort to start breathing normally. Then he realized that wasn't why he was holding in the air. It was hard to breathe around her.

The fort looked almost like it had the last time Webb saw it: two roughly constructed plywood rooms held together by bent nails and construction glue. He pulled the tarp away and gestured for her to step inside.

"I'm not going in first," she said, taking a step back. "A homeless person might be living in there now."

"You're right," he said with a solemn air. "If I don't come back, tell my mom I was the one who broke her Hummel."

He tore the tarp away dramatically and ducked inside. It was stupid, but it made her laugh. She let out five raspy notes.

After poking around both rooms, Webb reached outside, offering to guide her in. Her hand slipped into his. He could feel his heart beating in his hand. He hoped she couldn't feel his excitement through his skin.

"What the hell is a Hummel?" she asked.

"They're these expensive, creepy figurines that people collect. I don't know. My grandma gave it to her," Webb said.

Webb unfolded two mangled lawn chairs and rattled the dust off them.

"Is this what we do here?" Bree asked, taking a seat.

"Did you bring your comic books?"

"I don't like comic books."

"What do you like?" he asked.

She reached for a twig on the ground and started to draw shapes in the dirt.

"I'm really into Green Day recently. I used to be obsessed with the Red Hot Chili Peppers. I still like them, but not as much as The Killers or Foo Fighters. I would totally date Dave Grohl."

Webb nodded. "Me too. I love his beard," he teased.

"You guys would be perfect together!" Bree said with a smile. She reached into her purse and pulled out a bag of peanut M&Ms.

"Want one?" she asked.

"Sure."

She picked out the blue one and handed him the rest.

He felt brave in the fort, maybe because he had built it, or maybe because Bree thought it was cool. Whatever the reason, for the first time since he met her, he could talk to her the way he talked to his friends.

She dropped the stick and put her head in her hand and examined him. "How didn't I see it before, Webb Turner?"

"What?" His confidence evaporated.

"How funny and cute you are. You look kinda like Jude Law," she said and then smiled a new smile, one he hadn't catalogued yet.

He was sure she saw the blush stain his throat as it crept up to his cheeks.

"Come here," Bree said.

Webb froze, unsure what to do once he got there, or where to stand or sit.

"Come on," she pleaded.

He walked over and stood in front of her. She hooked her fingers in his belt loops.

"All the way down."

He kneeled on the ground. His head was almost level with hers. Only inches between their faces. He held each breath and let it out slowly so she wouldn't notice its weight, but his lungs begged for more oxygen.

"You shouldn't wear your hair so short in the front," she said. "It makes your forehead look big."

He held his palm against his hairline.

"Are your eyes green or brown? I can't tell."

"Hazel," Webb said, hoping his breath smelled ok. She was so close to him. Closer than he'd been since that first car ride.

"That's what hazel eyes look like?" She seemed surprised. Webb blinked. His eyes were dry from holding them open.

"Why don't you like to talk to me?" she asked. "Do you think I'm a bitch or something?"

"What? No." Why was she saying such a crazy thing? Didn't she know?

She moved closer. "It's like you're afraid of me. Are you?" Her breath smelled like peanuts.

"No. Maybe," he blurted.

She pushed her lips into his cheek. Warm. Rough and chapped in spots. His stomach dropped like it did on the gravity ride at the Clearfield County Fair.

"Was that scary?" she asked, pulling away.

Webb wanted to say "yes" and cup his palm over his face and never let the feeling escape, but he shook his head instead.

If he didn't do something right then, he would replay the regret forever.

He reached for her face and leaned in. As soon as their lips touched, she backed away.

"We should go before my mom calls to see if we made it to Merilee's."

Webb sat back down on the ground, afraid to stand up and show how he felt about the kiss. He thought about peaches. No, green beans. *Eww, Grandma.* He did math.

"Sure." He pivoted around to stand. It didn't matter. She was already outside.

"Does your mom like her job?" she asked when they made it back to the road.

Webb searched for his bearings. "Which one?"

"At the salon. She's a hairdresser, isn't she?"

"She's a stylist," Webb corrected, finally finding a piece of solid ground. "But she also sells makeup at the mall. I guess she likes it."

"Do you think she'd let me be her assistant?"

Webb couldn't believe they were talking about his mom and hair. He wanted to talk about the kiss, talk about what it might mean for them. He wanted to kiss her again.

"I can ask her."

"That's ok. I'll ask her," Bree said, walking faster ahead.

CHAPTER SIX - GLEN HOPE, PENNSYLVANIA

March 17, 2007

Only one person noticed they were late.

"Did you get lost?" Jason asked Bree, not Webb.

"We stopped by the fort on the way. It's pretty cool."

Jason shot an appraising glare at Webb. Webb answered with a noncommittal shrug, but he was sure Jason could see the heat map of Bree's kiss on his face.

"It's still standing," Webb said.

Merilee bounced over to them. "Hey, guys! Webb, did you see the food?" she asked, overly buoyant.

"No," he said, wondering why she was talking to him. Not that they didn't talk, but she never sought him out for conversation.

"You have to see it!" she said, grabbing his arm.

As Merilee steered him through the crowd, Webb looked back and caught a twinge of something in Bree's expression. It was a new look: jealousy.

Merilee let go when they arrived at the steps, like she finally trusted him to keep following her. Her blonde hair was spun into a thousand tight curls, except for her bangs. She'd straightened them.

No matter how hard Webb tried to see Merilee like someone new, he couldn't forget her brace-faced, awkward times. To new eyes, Merilee could be considered pretty. Her round face was thinning out; she was growing into her cheeks. He was surprised he hadn't noticed until now.

"My mom dyed everything green!" Merilee pointed out the green-tinted potato chips, Rice Krispie treats, French onion dip, shamrock cookies, and pasta salad. Webb didn't want to say it looked disgusting. She seemed so proud of it.

Merilee ladled some frothy green punch into a cup and handed it to him. He sniffed it. "It's Hi-C with some lime sherbet," she said.

"Thanks." He took a sip to be polite. It wasn't bad.

"So, are you going to prom?" Merilee asked like she didn't really care, but Webb sensed she was anxious for his response.

"I wasn't planning to," he said, reaching for a cookie. "What about you?" He didn't care about her answer. He wanted to go back downstairs to see where Bree was, who she was talking to, what kind of face she was making.

Merilee looked down and shrugged one shoulder. "No one's asked me yet. I'll probably tag along with Jason and Bree. My mom's driving us."

Webb perked up. If they all went together, he'd have an excuse to hang out with Bree all night.

"We could go together," Webb said before really thinking it through.

Merilee smiled. "Yeah, that would be cool," she said, her voice rising at the end of each word. "I should get back to my party. Help yourself to whatever." She rushed off to broadcast the news of their date.

He leaned back on the refrigerator and took a bite out of the cookie. It disintegrated into powder inside his mouth.

He suddenly regretted the decision and wanted to spit it out.

Just as Webb was going back downstairs, Jason loped into the kitchen with his cousins, Brent and Chris. Webb had met them a few times, but Brent didn't seem to remember.

"Man, this is kind of disgusting," Jason said, surveying the neon food.

"At least she didn't pick things that were naturally green, like your mom would," Webb said. "Here's some puréed spinach, kids." He made his voice go as high as he could.

Brent and Chris, who were on either side of Webb, laughed in stereo.

"That's funny," Brent said, or maybe it was Chris. Webb forgot who was who. "Your mom is so granola. I swear she said that at Christmas."

Jason flipped all three of them off just as Merilee's mom walked into the kitchen.

She gasped. "Jason Matthews!"

Suddenly sheepish, Jason shoved his hands in his pockets and whispered a quick apology to Mrs. Davis. The four of them slunk downstairs, holding in their snorts of laughter until they were back in the crowded basement.

Underneath the chatter, Kelly Clarkson invited them to break away. Webb scanned the room until he saw Bree standing by the air hockey table next to Merilee's older brother, Pete. He wanted to find an excuse to join them without becoming Pete's next casualty.

"So this is a party in No Hope?" Brent asked, plopping down on the scratchy plaid couch in the corner.

"Don't act like Tyrone is better," Jason said, turning defensive.

"At least we have a Burger King and a Sheetz," Chris offered.

"Sheetz *is* a mark of civilization," Webb agreed.

"It's a convenience store," Jason deflected, but they all knew Webb was right.

A victorious whoop from Pete interrupted their debate. "Who's next?" he boomed.

Bree waved a beckoning hand in their direction. At first Webb thought it was meant for him, but Jason stood. Before he left, he said, "At least we have hot girls."

As Jason took his place across from Pete, Webb wished he could be good at something. He wanted Bree to look at him like she was looking at Jason now.

"We should cover this song," Chris suggested. Webb strained to listen. Between clicks of the puck, he heard Journey's "Don't Stop Believin'."

"That's a stupid idea," Brent said. "This song's ancient. If the band has to do covers, they're going to be from this century."

"I don't know. A cover of this song would be different," Webb said. He could hear possible variations for the tempo and melody. He hummed them.

"Yes! Exactly. He gets it," Chris said, slapping alternative drum fills on his knees. "Do you play anything?"

"My grandma made me play violin in elementary school."

"You should join our band. We need someone on lead guitar."

"Guitar and violin aren't the same," Brent said.

Chris ignored his brother's protest. "It has strings. He could learn."

Being a guitarist in a garage band had to trump winning a game of air hockey.

On the other side of the room, Merilee joined the crowd at the air hockey table. He couldn't hear what she announced to the group, but he knew she was talking about him. Seconds later, Bree was heading his way.

"What do you think you're doing?" she asked.

Brent and Chris raised their eyebrows. Webb shifted, feeling cool that he had drama in common with her. He played dumb, like she was overreacting.

"Joining a band," he answered.

"Can I talk to you?" she asked.

In his head, he said, *not right now*, but he stood to follow her up the half flight of stairs and outside. Dusk stole the warmth of the afternoon, leaving them shivering and coatless on Merilee's front porch.

"Are you seriously going to Junior Prom with Merilee?"

"Yeah, why not? Does she have herpes or something?"

"How would I know?" Bree turned away, looking at the shaft of light stretching across the driveway from the porch. "Do you think she's pretty?"

"I guess so."

She didn't say anything. She didn't even look at him before she turned inside and left him alone on the porch. He entertained the thought of going back in, but he started to walk home instead. He wasn't going to play her game, even if he would be a willing participant in any other game he could play with Bree.

CHAPTER SEVEN - VERIZON CENTER, WASHINGTON, D.C.

January 22, 2016

For a second, Webb panicked. What song was next? Was he supposed to start it? The lights onstage dimmed, and Brent moved over to a piano that was hidden until now. The crowd waited for a clue. None of their songs had piano. You could almost hear the audience guessing.

High and low notes fought for attention as the familiar melody rang out.

"Just a small town girl, livin' in a lonely world. She took the midnight train goin' anywhere…" Brent sang.

Chris had suggested adding the Journey cover to the set list—an homage to their beginning. Brent and Garrett had protested, but for once, Chris won.

Webb let his fingers remember the progression. His body fought every movement. He never had to overcome a force this strong to play before—not even when he had the flu in Brazil.

At the beginning of the second verse, an agile girl scrambled on stage and ran toward Webb. The security guards flew out from the wings of the stage and grabbed her. As she kicked her feet in protest, her eyes connected with Webb's.

"Wait!" he yelled, raising his hand from the strings.

He knew those eyes, the tangle of blonde hair. But she didn't look like that anymore. He shook off the feeling of hope. Security yanked the girl offstage. Webb searched for the melody he was supposed to be playing.

He didn't know how he made it to the end of the song. As soon as it ended, the crowd blurred and his saliva soured. He escaped offstage just in time to throw up.

CHAPTER EIGHT - GLEN HOPE, PENNSYLVANIA

March 18, 2007

Webb tossed in bed, annoyed by the clang of dishes and laughter downstairs. He pulled a t-shirt over his sleep-matted hair and went to investigate. His mom was in the kitchen with Mrs. Brewer, who had brought over fresh-baked cinnamon rolls.

Bree was sitting at the small breakfast table. Suddenly, Web was embarrassed by the cracked brown linoleum and orange countertops. Here in his kitchen she looked like the Hope Diamond at a yard sale. A stream of sunlight hit something around her neck. Jason's ring dangled from a thin gold chain.

He patted his hair down over his forehead. It was too late to go back and brush his teeth and change out of his basketball shorts. He had to face her, morning breath and all.

"Hey," Webb said in a way that addressed them all.

Not knowing what to do with himself, he strode over to the refrigerator and pulled out a carton of orange juice. Maybe after getting the taste of sleep out of his mouth, he'd be able to look at her.

"Guess what?" Webb's mom said. "Bree's going to be my assistant at the salon."

Webb looked at his mom and then back at Bree. In a fleeting thought, he noticed how similar they were. Bree didn't say anything. She unwound her cinnamon roll, examining Webb from the corner of her eye. He wondered if she was going to bring up the fact that he'd left her at the party the night before.

"Cool," Webb said. "Hey, Mom, can I take out some of my birthday money?"

"For what?" She used her best "I'm a good mother" tone.

"I thought I'd go to the music store and get a guitar."

"Why don't you get Uncle Rick's guitar from grandma's attic?" his mom suggested. "It's free."

Webb shrugged. He didn't want to complain in front of Bree. It wouldn't really be free. His uncle's guitar would cost him a whole Saturday of chores for his grandma that started when he got there and ended with a dinner of rubbery, homemade Salisbury steak.

He hated Salisbury steak.

Bree followed her mother to the front door, hesitating when she reached the threshold. When her mother was out of earshot, she turned back.

"Where did you go last night?"

"I was bored, so I left," he said.

"Oh." She lingered in the doorway for a beat and then followed her mom across the street.

He watched her from behind the screen door, wishing he could ask her what she was thinking, why she had kissed him, if she really liked Jason. When Bree and her mom had disappeared behind their front door, Webb went back to the kitchen and called his grandma.

CHAPTER NINE - GLEN HOPE, PENNSYLVANIA

March 18, 2007

Webb's grandma was young enough to pass as his mother. Only a few streaks of grey highlighted her cropped and permed hair. But her youth didn't stop her from needing help with everything.

Since his grandpa died, she had been helpless to perform the smallest task that his grandfather used to do: putting things in the attic, installing the window air conditioners in the spring, coating the windows with plastic in the fall, raking leaves. Those chores all fell on Webb's stepdad or Webb. Lately, only on Webb.

The guitar was a small payment for the Saturday afternoons he'd spent unscrewing light covers and shaking fly corpses into the trash.

Today, his chores were simple: bring the Easter baskets down from the attic and clean up the sticks that had fallen in the yard.

"They'll put me in a home the second they think I can't take care of this house," she confided as Webb climbed up into the attic.

"No one's putting you in a home, Grandma. You're only fifty-two," Webb said.

"Fifty-seven," she corrected. "It's no fun getting old," she called up to him.

He dug through boxes bursting with Christmas decorations and old clothes. He waded away from the island of plywood that circled the hatch.

Balancing on the rafters, he made his way to the far end of the attic. Under an old hobby horse, Webb saw a scuffed brown guitar case. He wiggled it free and dragged it to a place illuminated by the single bulb in the middle of the attic.

Webb poked his head through the hatch. "Whose guitar is this?"

"Oh, that's your Uncle Rick's from when he was your age," she said.

"Do you think I could borrow it?" He crossed his fingers.

"Oh, I don't care. It's probably warped from being up there all these years. Did you find the Easter baskets?"

Webb pumped his fist in celebration and continued his search for the baskets. Just as he was about to give up, he saw a woven green-and-yellow-plastic handle peeking out from a box on the other side of the attic. He carefully threw the baskets down into the hallway and handed the guitar to his grandma waiting below.

He rested the case on the coffee table and opened it. A rough, wood-grained Alvarez acoustic was tucked inside the furry maroon interior. Webb eased out the guitar and cradled it in his lap.

"Your uncle was a natural," she said. "He could have really done something..." Her words trailed off.

Webb knew how her thought ended. His uncle could have done something if heroin hadn't flooded his veins and stolen the brightness of his life.

Webb curled his fingers around the neck, pressing down on random frets. It couldn't be that much different than the violin, could it? He gave a tentative strum. The strings shook wrong notes throughout the room.

"Those strings must be fifteen years old," his grandma said. "You'll have to get new ones. Go ahead and get washed up for dinner."

His grandma's dining room table was already set for two when he came out of the bathroom. Webb sat obediently at one of the chairs, ready to choke down the under-seasoned, gravy-slathered meat.

She spooned some on his plate and took a half portion for herself without gravy. Limp, canned green beans formed a crescent along the side of the plate. Webb scooped them into his mouth, getting it over with.

"Are you gonna tell your grandma what's new?"

Webb took a big bite to occupy his mouth and shrugged.

"Any girls?" she pressed. Webb wanted to talk about *her*. He wished he could confide in someone who might be able to help solve the enigma, but he wimped out at the last second.

"I'm going to the prom with Merilee Davis," he said.

"I know," she said, hiding a smile. "Her mom's on the bazaar committee at church. We met this morning."

"Oh, right," he said, chewing a chunk of ground steak.

"Well, I think it's great. Merilee is a nice girl, and pretty."

"I don't want to talk about this anymore, Grandma," he said.

She reached into her pocket, pulled out a wad of money, and pushed it across the table. "Buy yourself a nice outfit and some flowers for her."

Webb tucked it into his pocket and said, "Thanks."

"You're a good kid, Webster."

He spooned the last forkful into his mouth so he wouldn't have to respond.

CHAPTER TEN - GLEN HOPE, PENNSYLVANIA

March 19, 2007

They were connected at the mouth at the bus stop, on the bus, and now part of Jason's shoulder rested right against Webb's locker while his tongue swept inside Bree's mouth. They had to be doing it to torture him. Their lockers were rows away from Webb's.

Webb thought about shoving Jason out of the way so he could get his books, but he decided to tell Ms. Campbell he'd left his essay at home.

As he walked to his next class, he spotted Merilee down the hall, hidden in a clump of hairspray and lip gloss. He liked her. His grandma was right. She was a nice girl. She wouldn't kiss him and then take his best friend's ring an hour later. She probably wouldn't kiss him at all.

Merilee is a nice girl, Webb repeated in his head as he pushed through the crowded hallway.

"Hey, Webb," she said, smiling at first, then hiding it to play cool.

"So what does your dress look like?"

"It's light pink with some white sequins on the top, then the bottom kinda flares out... am I supposed to tell you this?"

Webb shrugged. "Am I supposed to understand all that?" He laughed. "Light pink should be enough for me to go on."

He shoved his hands into his pockets. He had never asked a girl to be his girlfriend. Really, before the other day, he had never asked a girl for anything more than a pencil. But Merilee seemed safe, comfortable, convenient. He looked down at his shoes, hoping to find the same bravery he had in the fort with Bree.

"Would you... do you want to go out with me?" he blurted.

The bell rang, and the stragglers scattered. The halls were almost empty.

"Oh, shoot! I'm going to be late," she said, running past him down the hall. He watched her almost wipe out on the glossy waxed floors. Webb didn't move. He didn't want to leave his invitation hanging in the air.

Before she turned into her classroom, she yelled back, "Yes."

By lunch, it seemed like everyone knew about Webb and Merilee—probably all one hundred and twenty-eight of his classmates.

When he walked into the cafeteria, she was hovering at the door, waiting for him.

"There's a seat at our table," she said.

Webb looked over to where he and Jason usually sat. Bree was in his seat.

"Why don't we sit at my table?" Webb asked.

Merilee forced an uncomfortable smile. "That sounds good."

As they sat down, Merilee glanced nervously back at her usual table and waved to Tori. Webb settled in across from Bree, patting an invitation on the seat next to him. Merilee hesitated before finally perching on the edge of the round plastic disc.

Webb recorded how Bree's lips twisted when he slipped his hand into Merilee's. Bree's jealousy was enough to fuel his commitment. He offered his new girlfriend a French fry, wiggling it playfully in front of her mouth until she grabbed it with her teeth. Bree let out a groan and looked away.

A few minutes later, he slid his hand down Merilee's back and let it fall to a stop in the curve of her waist. She jumped with a giggle. Webb tickled her until she screeched.

Bree picked up her tray and marched it to the trash. She didn't come back.

CHAPTER ELEVEN - GLEN HOPE, PENNSYLVANIA

March 19, 2007

"I have a girlfriend," Webb announced at dinner.

"I know," his mom said. "Grandma told me. Oh, and speaking of Grandma, I picked up some strings for Uncle Rick's guitar. They're in my purse."

"No, I mean it's official."

The doorbell rang, interrupting his declaration.

Why was he telling her anyway?

His mom started to stand, but Webb stopped her. "I'll get it," he said.

Instead of protesting like she usually would, she sat back down.

When he pulled the door open, Bree was standing on his porch, clutching a pillowcase stuffed with clothes. Her head was down, and she didn't look at him. At first he thought she was still upset from his antics at the lunch table, but then he noticed her shoulders were shaking.

"Are you ok?"

She shook her head, still not looking up. He reached out, but she shrugged him away.

"Is your mom here?" she squeaked.

"Yeah. She's in the kitchen…"

HIS MOM and Bree had been upstairs for a while. He wanted to eavesdrop, to find out why Bree was crying. He'd never seen her look so fragile. Webb picked at his dinner, flipping through possible scenarios that might bring her to his door. When he had pulled apart the tips of every limp broccoli floret, he shoved them all in his mouth and put his plate in the dishwasher.

Webb climbed the stairs the same way he would when his stepdad was in one of his moods. He poked his head into the guest room and saw his mom sitting on the edge of the bed, alone. The water squeaked on in the bathroom.

"What's going on?" he whispered.

"She's going to stay here until Mrs. Brewer gets back from Ohio."

Webb didn't know where to start or what questions to ask. "Is she hurt?"

"She'll be fine." It was the tone she used when she was trying to convince herself.

The phone rang. Webb picked it up from the extension in the hall. "Hello?"

"Hello, Webster. This is Mrs. Brewer. I... have you seen Bree?"

"Yeah. She's here—in the bathroom." He wondered if he wasn't supposed to say that.

"Can I talk to your mom?"

Webb called for his mom. She picked it up in another room. Before Webb hung up, he heard Mrs. Brewer say, "Thank you for being there for us. Sometimes he goes off his meds..."

He waited until he heard Bree shuffle back to the spare room. After a few minutes, he knocked on the closed door, hoping for an invitation inside, but she was silent. He stood in the hall until it felt awkward and then went back to his room.

With only a wall between them, he tried to reach out to her another way. He picked up the guitar and the new pack of strings. He examined how the strings connected to the pegs and decided he'd need to ask someone to help put them on. He strummed out a few jangling strokes, but the door stayed shut through the night.

The next morning, they walked out to the bus stop together. Bree seemed normal, as if she hadn't spent most of the night crying.

"It's really nice of you guys to take me in for the next week," she said as they walked down the street.

"You're staying for a week?" Webb asked.

"I'll try not to get in your way," she said, cold, offended. She shifted her backpack to the other shoulder.

"I didn't mean it like that."

"It's fine. I don't want to make things uncomfortable for Merilee."

"Don't worry. You won't. Merilee and I have a pretty great relationship," he said.

From her expression, he could see that his words stung, like he hoped they would.

CHAPTER TWELVE - VERIZON CENTER, WASHINGTON, D.C.

January 22, 2016

What would happen if he left the show right now? A lawsuit? A fine? Maybe he could fake an illness. There was a clause for that.

If he had any allegiance left to the band, he might have thought harder about it. When Brent launched into a story about the next song, Webb placed the guitar on the stand. Without a look back, he walked off the stage.

Charlotte grabbed his jacket and yanked him back. "What the fuck are you doing? Get back out there!"

His canned reply of "Fuck off, Charlotte" wouldn't be enough to stop her from chasing him. In the harsh yellow lights, away from the stage and the energy of the crowd, Webb crumpled in on himself.

"I have to go."

"You have to wait until after the show. Go out there and finish it," Charlotte pleaded.

He stood up, letting his grief turn to anger. "She's dying, Char. I have to go."

"I know. I rented a car. Just finish the show, and we can go up together."

"I have to go now—alone."

Their eyes locked.

"Fuck," she said and clicked the button on her headset. "I need Vince onstage now to fill in for Webb. Tell the driver to pull around to Loading Dock C." She looked at Webb. "Promise me you'll be careful."

"Always. I promise," he said, tossing her the jacket on his way out.

IN THE few seconds that Webb had been outside, the shoulders of his sweat-soaked t-shirt were dusted white with wet flakes. As he climbed into the chauffeured car, his anxiety expanded, bubbling and pressing everything outward.

The driver wove through D.C., twisting through the short blocks, working his way through the maze of stout government buildings. Other than Pennsylvania Avenue, Webb didn't know much about the streets or the landmarks (except the obvious ones). They passed a Budget Rental Car office.

"Hey? Isn't that one back there?" Webb asked.

"Your boss wants me to get you out of the city before letting you drive, and besides, they're closed. You like football?" the driver asked.

"Sure, sometimes," Webb lied.

"I had someone in my cab yesterday who told me that they're going to change the Redskins' name. Do you know what they are going to rename them?"

The driver waited for Webb to respond. "Uh, no. What?" he asked finally.

"The Washington Deadskins," the driver said, belting out a squeaky laugh. "The Washington Deadskins."

He repeated the punchline a few more times, laughing like someone who had told the joke for the first time. Webb clutched his abdomen, trying to stop the weight inside from dragging him all the way into despair.

They crossed the river and stopped in front of a Camaro idling in a no-parking zone.

"I hope that's not your car," the driver said, ticking his tongue. "Rear-wheel drive is not good in the snow."

Webb didn't care what piece of wheeled metal would get him home. The only thing he cared about was closing the distance between D.C. and Glen Hope.

A scrawny twenty-something kid with acne scars approached him.

"The lady who called said to give you something with four-wheel drive, but I thought you'd like this better."

"Thanks," Webb said. "So do I have to sign anything?"

The attendant held out a paper. "Just this," he said sheepishly, and then added, "I wanted to go to the show tonight, but I couldn't get off work."

Webb smiled. "What's your name?"

"Alex."

Webb scribbled.

Alex,

Everything happens for a reason.

Webb Turner

The GPS already had directions loaded onto the screen.

CHAPTER THIRTEEN - GLEN HOPE, PENNSYLVANIA

March 24, 2007

Having Bree around turned out to be more of a disruption than Webb anticipated. With her in his house, he couldn't stop thinking about her. It made him think before he did anything. What would she think about the TV show he picked, or how he chewed his meatloaf, or how long he was in the bathroom?

Webb's mom had to work late that night. She bought two frozen dinners for them. His stepdad wouldn't be home until tomorrow. They were alone. Completely alone.

"Which one do you want?" he asked, holding out the Hungry Man dinners for her to examine. Fried chicken and Salisbury steak. She picked the chicken, but Webb didn't mind. He'd eat Salisbury steak for her.

"Do you have any movies?" she asked as he cut a slit in the plastic wrapper over the mashed potatoes.

"There are a few in the cabinet next to the TV," he said, placing the chicken dinner in the microwave.

"I'll pick something and put it on while you make dinner," she teased.

When steam was spitting out from the splits in the cellophane, Webb set their meals on the coffee table. Bree plopped on the couch, her legs tucked under her in a crisscross, her hair flopping on the top of her head in a sloppy bun. He recorded the look on her face: happy and relaxed.

He knew what she had picked as soon as the movie started. It wasn't hard to guess; they only owned ten movies.

"Nice choice," Webb said.

He would have chosen *Top Gun* too.

As the movie played and they finished their frozen dinners, Bree moved closer. By the time Goose went down, she was curled into his chest. It happened organically, as if it was supposed to happen exactly like that. After a few minutes of silence, she looked up at Webb.

"Do you really like her?"

"Merilee? Yeah, she's a nice girl."

Bree sat up, pushing herself off Webb's chest. "Is that what you want? A nice girl?"

The sincerity in her voice confused him at first, and then it made him angry. He didn't want to confront her about it, especially since she was in such a fragile state, but he didn't want to let the unanswered questions hang between them anymore.

"I don't get you. You kiss me and then start going out with my best friend an hour later? Now you're doing… this? What do you want, Bree?" The volume of his voice startled them both.

Her face hardened. "I want to move out of my parents' house. To get away from here."

"That's not what I meant."

"I don't know what I want," she blurted and then looked away. "I mean, I know what I want, but I don't."

"That doesn't even make sense," Webb said, pushing himself up from the couch. He didn't know where he would go, but he wanted to leave the room, maybe even the house, the state, the country.

Then she was at his side. Her fingers trailed down his arm until she found his hand.

"I'm really messed up."

"You don't think everyone is messed up?"

"Not like me."

He held his breath, hoping she would tell him, but she looked down like she was embarrassed.

"I don't care if you think you're messed up; I think you're perfect," he confessed.

"I'm definitely not perfect."

"Give me one example."

She tugged on her sleeves and pulled them over her hands. "I'm the reason he's hurt," she whispered.

"How?"

"After he lost his arm, he was pissed off all the time. He was chasing me. I ran into the kitchen. My mom had the deep fryer on the island counter, but the cord was plugged into the wall…"

Webb touched her arm as he gathered words that might make her feel better. He settled on, "You can't blame yourself for an accident."

"That's easy for you to say. He thinks I did it on purpose."

"Well, you'll never have to worry about what he thinks when we're famous," Webb said, hoping to defuse the seriousness.

"I guess everything happens for a reason," she said.

He sat back down and made a place for her in the crook of his arm. She curled in. Webb wished he could fast-forward to a future where they would be together like this all the time.

CHAPTER FOURTEEN - I-495, MCLEAN, VIRGINIA

January 22, 2016

It wasn't until he got on the highway that Webb thought about how long it had been since he'd driven.

Seven years.

He stayed safely in the right lane, but even that was moving faster than he was comfortable driving in good conditions. In a few hours, he'd be confronting the sharp roads that twisted through the mountains. Webb tried to remember the streets, the shortcuts, the landmarks. He wondered what had changed, if he would still feel suffocated there.

He fumbled with the touchscreen, trying to make it play some music to help him stop thinking. He had to focus on driving, on getting there, not about the consequences of walking out of a show at the Verizon Center.

He wanted to stop at a gas station, but none of the exits looked like they had an easy way to get to a convenience store or fast food. He'd probably have to wait until he was farther away from the city. He didn't want to wait too long, though.

Aside from the steady snow, it seemed easier to drive now that he was on the highway. Maybe there were fewer people on the road, or maybe he was remembering how to anticipate what other cars were going to do, or maybe it was exactly the same, but he lacked the energy to be nervous anymore.

The adrenaline of performing had worn off, and now his eyes were heavy. He needed coffee and maybe a cigarette. He'd quit smoking a few months ago, but he felt like smoking now. There wasn't anything to distract him.

He pressed enough buttons, and the radio finally came on. NPR. The soft voice pulled at his eyelids like a weight. Next station. Norah Jones crooned, "Come away with me…" His hand returned to the wheel, and he pushed the gas pedal down harder.

CHAPTER FIFTEEN - GLEN HOPE, PENNSYLVANIA

March 24, 2007

Bree stirred as Webb pulled his arm out from under her. She had fallen asleep, but he had to get ready.

"Where are you going?"

"Merilee's older brother is taking us to Irvona."

"Oh." He could tell she was disappointed. Jason had an away game in Patton.

"Are you going to be ok alone here?" he asked.

"I'll call Hailey and see if I can go to her house."

"That sounds like a good idea." He didn't want to leave her.

She stood up. They were face-to-face, and Bree's fingers fumbled at the hemline of his shirt until she was able to slide them underneath. Webb inhaled. Her fingers were cold on the naked skin of his abdomen. They inched up at first and then swept quickly around to his back.

"What are you doing?" he whispered in staggered breaths. She didn't answer; instead, she squeezed.

"Hugging you," she said into his chest.

HE DIDN'T remember how to act. For the last few hours, he had existed in a strange world—somewhere between reality and every hopeful dream he'd ever had. It was a place he didn't want to leave, but he had to face his girlfriend.

He hoped Merilee couldn't read the guilt that consumed him. It was silly to think he might look different from a hug, but he felt like someone else.

When he came down, clean and oversaturated with cologne, Bree was studying a collection of dusty family photos on the wall next to the television, acting like nothing had happened.

"Who's this?"

Webb took a closer look. "That's my sister, Zoe."

"You have a sister?"

"She lives with my dad in Clearfield. We see her, like, once a year."

Webb didn't remember life with Zoe and his real dad. They only showed up in a picture or a story. Except for a few days a year, Zoe was a phantom, an old wives' tale, a family fact that you've always known but one you never think about hard enough to question.

"Why didn't you tell me you had a sister?"

"You don't tell me everything," he accused.

"Like what?"

"Like... why you're staying with us for a week."

She crossed her arms. "My dad's an asshole. He tried to kill me."

"Seriously?"

"Not really, but kind of." She rubbed her face, as if it would make Webb's question go away. She shot a glance at the window. "I think they're here."

Webb pulled back the curtain and saw a minivan approaching.

"Are you sure you don't want me to stay?"

"I told you. I'm going to call Hailey. We'll make some popcorn and watch TV. I'll be fine."

Webb hesitated at the threshold, wishing he could stay. Before he left, he said, "I'll bring you back some pizza."

CHAPTER SIXTEEN - IRVONA, PENNSYLVANIA

March 24, 2007

 Glen Hope didn't have a pizza place, or even a restaurant. People either went to Choo Choo's in Irvona or Pizza King in Coalport. Everyone had their preference. Webb preferred Pizza King because he hated the name "Choo Choo's." On any given weekend night, all the tables were full.

Merilee's brother Pete didn't sit with them. Webb was glad. Unless they were around adults, Pete refused to call Webb by name. He called him "dictionary," placing special emphasis on the "dick" so it sounded more like DICK-shinary.

They had their own table in the corner. They were out, being a couple, just like Merilee wanted. But the thought of Bree home alone made Webb too nervous to eat any pizza. All he could think about was going back as soon as he could.

Tomorrow he'd make pancakes, and they'd watch another movie, or do anything they felt like doing together. He had to break up with Merilee. He thought about doing it right then.

"My mom wants you to come over a little early so we can take pictures," Merilee said.

"For what?"

"Junior Prom?" She put down her slice of pizza. "Are you ok?

You seem weird."

He knew it. She could tell he was thinking about Bree. His guilt was tattooed in an invisible ink that only girls could read. Part of him wanted to confess that he was in love with Bree, but he knew he should wait until after the dance.

"I just remembered that I forgot to order your flowers."

She smiled with relief. "That's all right. There's still time."

As he ate his pizza, Webb listened to Merilee babble about someone breaking up with someone else. The whole time, he pictured Jason and Bree getting into the fight she was describing. The waitress brought a slice of pepperoni to go. Webb waited for Merilee to ask who it was for, but she never did.

Pete drove them home and dropped Webb off on the way. It may have been the first time Webb was happy that there wasn't a lot to do near Glen Hope.

Even though he wanted to run, he took his time on the way to the front door. All the lights were on in the house, and his mom's car was in the driveway. It didn't matter, he just wanted to see her.

He thought maybe Bree would be sitting on the couch, but the living room was empty.

"Mom?" he called out.

"Up here."

He hopped up the stairs. The door to the guest room was open, and his mom was inside, stripping the bed. The room still smelled like Bree.

"What are you doing?" he asked, watching her shake a pillow out of its case.

"I'm getting the room ready, just in case." He knew to fill in the rest of her thought with *Just in case Zoe decides to come home.* Bree was gone.

"How was your day?" she said.

"It was…" Webb skipped through the confusing parts from the afternoon until he got to the date, Choo Choo's, the flowers. "Good, except I need to get a corsage for Merilee's dress. She said it's pink with white stuff or something."

"I can pick one up from the flower shop next to the salon."

"Thanks." He lingered in the doorway, hoping his mom would say something about Bree, but she continued to tuck the sheets into the mattress. "I'm going to go to bed now."

He wasn't tired at all, but he felt like he was on the verge of some emotion that required solitude.

"Goodnight," she said without looking at him.

Webb shut his door and stood, staring ahead. His eyes moved down the wall to his bed. A single pack of peanut M&Ms rested on his pillow. He picked up the guitar and mindlessly moved his hand up and down the neck, holding down different strings, seeing which notes went together. He sank his misery and hope into the sour notes. Brent was right. Playing guitar was nothing like the violin. The scales were different, and there were more strings. But Webb kept trying, just to prove Brent wrong.

CHAPTER SEVENTEEN - GLEN HOPE, PENNSYLVANIA

March 25, 2007

Webb looked at her house at least a dozen times the next morning. He hid in the slit of the curtains, just in case she decided to walk outside. It would be crazy of him to keep staring at her house all day. He decided to go to Cole's house.

He took the guitar with him. Cole had Wi-Fi, his own laptop, *and* a desktop. Last week, his parents gave him a cell phone. He was probably the richest kid Webb knew. Cole's mom stocked the pantry with Oreos, Doritos, and cases of soda. The Tates' house was everything Webb's house wasn't.

He placed the guitar on the couch and picked up a game controller. Cole didn't give him much time to get acclimated to the game before he started shooting him. Webb shot back, and they engaged in a quick struggle.

"Hey, can you look up how to put strings on my guitar after you kick my ass?" Webb asked.

"Sure," Cole said and blew Webb's head off.

"That was fast."

Cole pulled out his laptop and searched for tutorials. Ten minutes into trying to restring the guitar from a video Cole found online, Mr. Tate came downstairs. He unburied a beer from the second fridge.

Since he was trying to hide the beer from Mrs. Tate, Cole's dad looked for conversation with Webb and Cole while he drank it.

"That's a nice guitar. Can I see it?"

Webb handed it over. "We're trying to put new strings on it, but we can't figure out how to get the old strings off…"

"I can restring it." Cole's dad sat his beer on the end table and unwound the pegs until the strings became floppy. He untangled the tops. One by one, the old strings zipped off.

"Alright. Hand me the E string."

Webb searched the writing on each packet and presented Mr. Tate both envelopes that said "E."

"Crap. I got a bad pack."

"There are two E strings, a high and a low," Cole's dad said. "Give me the thicker of the two."

Webb peeked inside the paper pouches and handed over the larger E string. He watched Mr. Tate attach the new strings and then tune the guitar by ear. Cole started another game as his dad shared his knowledge of basic chords and a blues scale with Webb.

By the time Mr. Tate went back upstairs, Webb felt like he had pinched out lit matches with the pads of his fingers. They hurt so much, he had a hard time gripping the PlayStation controller, but he was filled with a new drive to learn every Green Day song he could.

CHAPTER EIGHTEEN - GLEN HOPE, PENNSYLVANIA

March 26, 2007

Webb couldn't wait to go to school. He wanted to look at her and make sure she was ok, but she didn't come out of her house at the regular time. Jason was already at the bus stop, though, waiting. His eyes lit up when Webb approached.

"Dude. You have no idea what went on last night," he said, even before Webb was at the stop sign where their streets crossed.

Webb didn't ask or even acknowledge him.

Unfazed by the silence, Jason leaned closer. "We fucked," he whispered and then gave Webb a proud smile.

"Wait. Who?"

"Bree, who else? She climbed into my bedroom window after the game and practically jumped me."

At that same moment, Bree rounded the corner. Webb's throat constricted at the sight of her.

"Shit. I forgot my homework," he said and bolted back toward his house. He stayed on the other side of the street so he wouldn't have to look Bree in the eyes.

When he got inside, he called his mom at the salon and told her that his stomach hurt. Technically, it was the truth.

He stripped out of his school clothes, curled back in bed, and hoped the act of compacting his body would somehow fuse his shattered insides back together.

A few hours passed. There was only so much time he could spend lying in agony. He picked up the guitar and worked on the scales Mr. Tate had taught him the day before. He played until he forgot time, forgot school, forgot her. He started to sing. The pain dissolved.

At three o'clock, the phone rang. Webb didn't answer. A few minutes later, the doorbell rang. He ignored it. Then the knocking started. Webb trudged downstairs and opened the door. Bree was there.

"Did you leave something here?"

"No. I… I just want to talk to you."

"I can't talk right now."

"I feel like you're mad at me. Are you?"

"No, I'm busy." He wanted to tell her the truth, that she'd destroyed every organ in his body, but he was afraid if he started talking, he might cry or throw something.

She played with the sleeve of her hoodie and pursed her lips. She was probably searching for another to lie to trick him into letting her in a little deeper.

"Webb, please. Let me explain," she said, not sincere enough to be begging.

"I have homework to do."

"But you didn't go to school…"

The door rocked in his hand as he stepped back into his living room.

"See you around."

He watched her walk across his front yard. But instead of going home, she turned down the road to Jason's house.

He fell into his bed, letting his regret pull him deeper into the sinking spot in the middle of his mattress. He stared straight up until the shapes of the plaster ceiling started to move.

When he finally got bored, he picked up his guitar and played the song he'd written over and over. As the sun sank lower in his window, he changed lyrics, added a bridge, and transferred all of his confusion and pain to the notes and the words. It was a terrible song, but writing it had made him feel better.

CHAPTER NINETEEN - ROUTE 70, SOMEWHERE OUTSIDE FREDERICK, MARYLAND

January 22, 2016

If he hadn't left his phone on the bus, he would have called his mom to let her know he was on his way—to see if Bree was still alive. He pulled off the highway, chose the emptiest gas station from the four options at the exit, and braced himself for recognition.

Even out of context, there was always one fan who recognized him. It didn't matter if he was wearing sunglasses and a baseball cap.

Charlotte said being a mentor on a songwriting reality show would be a good career move, and it was. Brent's shadow didn't eclipse him anymore. But after the show's first season, there were always whispers, fingers pointing at him, and for the bravest fans, a few selfies.

Webb hardly had enough energy to continue the journey; there was no way he could put on a smile for a fan. Aisle by aisle, he searched for things he might need for the next two and a half hours. Two cans of Red Bull, a bottle of water, some beef jerky, and peanut M&Ms. He dumped his selections on the counter, afraid to make eye contact with the cashier. She was in her forties, overweight, smiling.

"Anything else?" she asked.

Don't ask for cigarettes. Don't ask for cigarettes.

"Is there a pay phone around here?"

She snorted. "I haven't seen a pay phone since... I don't know when." She squinted. He could tell she was trying to figure out how she knew him. Webb patted around for his wallet and threw down a twenty. At least he didn't leave his wallet on the bus.

Before she could begin counting his change, he was out the door and running back to the car. He turned the ignition and sat there, holding the M&Ms.

The sharp sadness sped from his stomach until it reached his eyes. As he clutched the bag tighter and the windshield fogged, Webb contemplated not going any farther. If he stayed here and didn't see her and never spoke to his mom again, maybe he could believe Bree was alive and happy somewhere.

THE RED Bull finally kicked in. As he approached Frederick, it started to snow again. The roads gradually grew steeper. His foot was completely comfortable on the gas pedal now, and he wove between cars with a mechanical ferocity. Concentrating on breaks in the traffic kept his mind clear. There was a rhythm to it, a meditation. And above all, it was something else to focus on.

Under the engine noise, the DJ talked about the snow in terms of feet. But even with the threat of the growing blizzard, Webb couldn't keep his thoughts away from what might happen when he got there. He tried a few opening lines out loud.

"There's something you should know... That sounds stupid." He started over. "Hey. I missed you. You still look beautiful." He shook his head, too embarrassed to hear his own words.

The cars ahead of him started to slow as the wind picked up. As he pictured the scene, he realized he didn't even know where she was. He'd been so focused on getting to Pennsylvania, he hadn't bothered to find out his final destination. A hospital? Her house? In hospice?

He had to find a phone and hope that something out here in the rolling farmland would be open at this hour. Webb pressed the GPS, flashing his eyes to the screen at quick intervals until he found each option. He held down voice command, asked for the nearest Walmart, and let the car lead him there. There might not be pay phones anymore, but he could buy a disposable phone.

In the parking lot, icy slush lurked beneath two fluffy inches of powder. He tried to run to the door, but he slid, forcing slush into his shoe. He shook his foot, trying to stop the cold wetness from creeping down his ankle, but it only pushed it in deeper.

Inside, the fluorescent lights burned Webb awake. Between the ultra-white floors and blue signs, he had to squint to see the world he'd spent the last seven years forgetting. He'd grown so accustomed to people doing things for him, to being oblivious about the details that built his days. Now, he was awkwardly navigating a discount store, looking for a prepaid phone.

The late-night customers stared at him. He probably looked like an alien with his sinewy limbs, vintage t-shirt, and New York haircut. He knew how bizarre he looked to them, a strange creature walking among the Cartwright jackets and camouflage.

He wanted to tell them that he was one of them until he realized it would be a lie. He had completely left the life where he'd make a midnight Walmart run after the third shift.

Webb kept his head down as he marched toward the back of the store. He didn't want to waste too much time picking out a phone. Although he only needed it for one or two calls, he agonized over the different plans and packages. Which ones were immediately active?

He looked around for someone in a blue vest. A group of college kids brushed past him, heading toward the video games. He knew they might recognize him, but he had no other choice.

"Hey man, do you know anything about these things?" he asked the tallest kid who was trailing behind his friends.

"Yeah, I've used them before…"

A TempFive T-shirt with Webb's face in the top corner peeked out from under the kid's wrinkled button-down. Webb waited for him to say what a big fan he was, but they were kneeling there for a minute, and the kid didn't seem to catch on.

The need to be recognized started building in his chest. Not from a place of ego—Webb was starting to wonder if he was still alive. He was so used to being someone. But on the road by himself, Webb hardly had an identity. He felt absolutely invisible.

He thanked the kid and carried the refill card and phone to the register. Then he heard, "Dude. I just helped Webb Turner pick out a TracPhone."

In the parking lot, he wrestled with the phone for ten minutes before he could finally make a call. To do this, press this… Webb almost gave up.

The line kept ringing on the other end; his mom probably wasn't home. Webb couldn't remember her cell number. He couldn't remember any numbers other than ones he learned when he was in elementary school: his home phone, his grandmother's phone, and Jason's. Charlotte would know it, but he didn't know her number either, or how to call information. How did he become so helpless and inept at life?

If it wasn't such a pain in the ass to set up the phone, he would have stomped it out of existence with his foot. He wished he'd bought a pack of cigarettes.

An answering machine picked up. His mom's voice asked callers to leave a message.

"I left my phone in D.C., so if you get this, I'm on my way."

Webb sat for a moment and closed his eyes, searching for any thread of peace. He had to keep going. The only thing he could do was to shrink the distance, one mile at a time, for the next two and a half hours.

CHAPTER TWENTY - GLEN HOPE, PENNSYLVANIA

March 30, 2007

Webb hadn't talked to Bree since she left his porch. The next day, her mom had come home, and everything returned to normal—everything except Webb. His heart had calcified. Now it hung in his chest like ore.

A light pink corsage chilled in his refrigerator, and a matching tie clung to the shoulder of his suit, waiting to be forced into a knot around his neck. The dance had to be perfect. From now on, Webb was going to be the ideal boyfriend. He just hoped Merilee would never find out that he and Bree had curled up together—that Bree had touched his bare stomach.

WEBB STAYED quiet in the backseat. They passed Bree's house. A flame of red silk slipped inside Jason's dad's car as they drove by, incinerating Webb's last hope that he could show Bree how little he cared about what she had done. Maybe that was why she had changed her mind about riding with them.

The high school was only twenty minutes away, but it seemed twice as long trapped in Mrs. Davis' van. Every few seconds, she'd shoot a glance in the rear-view mirror, which she had tilted so much, Webb doubted she could even see the road behind them.

Merilee didn't seem to mind. She chatted happily in a whisper. Occasionally Webb would nod or smile or say, "Uh-huh."

As they fell into the line outside the gym, Webb pulled out the tickets and tried to examine Merilee like he would have if Bree was his date. None of her quirky gestures seemed worthy of recording. Bree had thousands of expressions, but Merilee only had twelve.

The gym didn't look anything like the high-school dances in the movies. It was still very much a gym, the smell of stale sweat and floor wax. Swaths of crepe paper sagged, haphazardly taped to the bleachers and walls. There was no punch bowl to spike; instead the concession window they used for basketball games was open, throwing buzzing fluorescent light into the room.

Merilee walked toward a group of similarly dressed girls. Webb followed, casting his eyes casually around the room, searching for a hint of red among the pale pinks and electric blues.

He stood next to Merilee, wondering why he had wanted to come to this stupid dance in the first place. He didn't care about dancing, or small talk, or socializing in general. The prospect of touching Merilee's waist or hands or lips wasn't enough to convince him that it was worth being here. He wanted to be back in his room, practicing guitar and writing songs.

Just as he was about to anchor himself to a table in the corner, Brent and Chris made their way across the gym toward their group.

"What are you doing here?" Webb asked.

"We met these chicks at the party. They asked us to the dance and we were like, 'Why the fuck not?'" Brent said.

Webb looked over at Merilee and her friends just as one of them whispered something and pointed over to Tori Jameson.

Merilee leaned to Webb and whispered, "Tori and Justin… I'll be right back," and ran across the gym to join the protective circle that was starting to form around Tori.

A few seconds later, Tori saw something that upset her even more and took off toward the bathroom. The rest of the pack followed.

"I'm not sure why they invited us," Webb said.

"I have something that will make this dance a little more entertaining. Who's in?" Brent asked, pulling out a joint, shaded in the cup of his hand. Webb looked for Merilee. When he confirmed that her dress was part of the cluster chasing after Tori, he shrugged and nodded.

Brent led them to the bathrooms—the opposite direction from the chaperones standing guard at the gym door.

"We can't smoke that in the bathroom," Webb protested.

"We're not going to," Brent said as they approached a door. It was one of those doors that became invisible because you weren't allowed to use it. Brent tried the knob, but it didn't move.

Chris stood with his back to his brother, acting like a barrier. He jerked his head in a motion for Webb to do the same.

"Plan B," Brent said, kneeling in front of the knob. He fished two tiny metal pieces from his pocket and slid them into the keyhole. After he wiggled them around for a few seconds, the lock popped.

They ducked into the coaching office. Webb quickly closed the door.

"How did you do that?" Webb asked.

"Our brother Greg is a locksmith. He taught us how to pick simple locks. We should be able to go out back by the football field."

They wound through the locker room and down the hall to the field. Webb gritted his teeth as Brent pushed his way outside, expecting to hear an alarm ring out, but nothing happened. In fact, it was so easy to sneak out that Webb was sure someone was waiting to catch them.

Brent lit the joint and took a few hits before passing it to Chris. Webb shoved his hands into his pockets, unsure if he was going to do it. He'd smoked stale cigarette butts that Jason had picked out of his dad's ashtray, but he'd never seen weed, much less smoked it. Chris shoved the pin joint his way. Webb took a hand out of his pocket and sucked in a hit, immediately coughing it all out.

Brent threw Webb a flask. He took a swig and immediately gagged on the body-warmed liquid inside. It tasted like water from a Christmas tree stand that had been microwaved for a few seconds.

"What is that?" Webb coughed even harder, trying not to retch.

"Gin. It's all our dad had in the liquor cabinet," Chris said, taking another drag off the joint.

Webb didn't feel anything yet except the compulsion to spit the pine coating from the back of his mouth. He reached for the joint when Chris was done and took a smaller drag. This time it stayed in, only scratching the back of his throat a little. They passed it around the circle until it was gone.

The herbal smoke still clung to the inside of Webb's nose as they traversed back through the locker room. He wondered if everything around them had absorbed the smell of weed, or if he was the only one who could smell it. He wondered if the hallway got longer? Had they been gone for hours? What if the dance was over?

"Dude, you ok?" Brent asked before they slid back into the bathroom.

"Wait. What?" Webb asked.

"He's so baked." Chris laughed.

The pounding beat from the dance bounced from the tile walls into Webb's chest, but the words were muffled. It was almost too loud. Webb couldn't imagine being in the gym where he was sure to be bombarded with the full-volume version of "Photograph" by Nickelback. Would it be weird if he stayed in the bathroom until the music stopped?

"I don't think I can go in there," Webb said, trying to sound cooler than he felt.

"You'll be fine. Music is so much better this way," Brent said.

They left the bathroom. The gym was thick with textured notes and swells. Webb swam in the pool of sound like it was the first time he had ever heard music.

It turned out he wasn't gone very long after all. Maybe ten minutes?

Webb expected Merilee to be waiting, worried after searching the gym for him, but she was coming out of the bathroom with the other girls. Chris handed out pieces of cinnamon gum as they made their way back to their dates. The spice of the gum burned his mouth and throat. He flipped it around with his tongue, hoping to spread out the spikes of pain.

"I'm so sorry," Merilee said as she leaned into Webb's chest, her face wrinkling with sincere apology and concern. "Tori just found out that Justin is dating Kylie Reicher. It's kind of a mess."

"Not a problem," Webb said. Kanye's "Gold Digger" pulled his head back and forth. He felt the beat everywhere. He reached for Merilee. "Come on. Let's dance."

She hesitated, casting a quick glance back at her friends before following Webb into the middle of the crowd.

Usually Webb would avoid dancing, but he had to move. Chris was right. The dance just got a lot more interesting. Webb didn't even like Kanye.

"Boulevard of Broken Dreams" came on next. The chorus kicked in, and Webb's body felt incendiary. He was going to make music like this. He was going to be the biggest fucking rock star ever.

CHAPTER TWENTY-ONE · GLENDALE HIGH SCHOOL, FLINTON, PENNSYLVANIA

March 30, 2007

Webb's hair stuck to his forehead. He and Merilee jumped to OutKast singing, "Hey Ya!" They were panting for air when it ended. The lights changed from zipping blue and green beams to the sparkles of the disco ball. Billie Joe's voice broke through about turning points and forks in the road.

Webb wiped his sweaty palm on his pants and pulled Merilee into him, hoping that Bree had noticed. Merilee rested her head on his shoulder, sweet, innocent. He held her and let his free hand rest on her back. His nose grazed her antiseptic-smelling hair.

Cheap hairspray.

As he tilted his head onto hers, a flash of red caught the corner of his focus. He pulled Merilee's chin up so he could kiss her. Her lips were tight, tense, bland.

When he opened his eyes, he saw Bree's back. She was walking out of the gym with Jason a few steps behind her. He could tell by her strides that she didn't plan on coming back.

MERILEE'S MOM was the first in the pick-up line. After the kiss, Merilee was giddier than Webb had ever seen her. She held Webb's hand tighter than before. He wished it meant more to him, but it didn't.

"Did you kids have a good time?" Mrs. Davis asked as they climbed in the minivan.

"Yeah, it was great," Webb said.

"Webb's a really good dancer," Merilee purred.

The dance changed things between Webb and Merilee. More specifically, the kiss changed things. In the back seat, she grabbed Webb's knee and inched her hand higher. He blocked it before she had the chance to grab anything meaningful.

"What?" she asked in a hushed whisper.

"Your mom's right there," he whispered back.

"She can't see anything," she said.

It was too dark to see her roll her eyes, but he could tell she did. Eventually she stopped fighting and let her hand rest as high on his thigh as he would let her go. The heat from her palm soaked through his khakis. He spent the rest of the ride hoping she'd move it away. It wasn't that he didn't want to be touched. It was just that he'd rather be touched by Bree.

CHAPTER TWENTY-TWO - I-70, OUTSIDE HAGERSTOWN, MARYLAND

January 23, 2016

 As the car climbed the mountain, Webb's ears clogged with the rising pressure. The closer he got to the summit, the harder the snow fell. The radio signal broke apart, so he turned it off. Just when he decided to figure out if the stereo had a satellite subscription, the car rang with a call. Webb touched the screen to answer, confused by how or why it was ringing.

"Hello?" Webb asked the empty car.

"How are you doing?"

It was Charlotte. Her voice hugged him through the car speakers.

"Fine. Confused. How are you calling me? I left my phone in my suitcase."

"Do you really think I'd put you in a car with no way to contact you? You always lose your phone, and you haven't driven in seven years."

Her words stuck a bandage over the gushing wound in his chest.

"So, any word?" she asked.

"I don't know anyone's phone numbers anymore. I called my house, but my mom's probably with her now."

"She is. Bree's in the ICU at UPMC Altoona."

Webb didn't want her to say "Fuck off" yet. He wanted her to talk him through the whole ride, but he didn't know how to ask.

"Hey, what song did they decide to close with?" he asked before she could hang up.

"Brent ended up choosing 'A Thousand Ways to Say I'm Sorry.'"

"He hates that song..."

"I guess he thought it was appropriate."

He didn't want to talk about Brent; he could only deal with one crisis at a time.

"Are you getting tired yet?" she asked, her voice getting lower, like she was tired too.

"I drank two Red Bulls. I think I'll be up all night."

"The snow is supposed to get really bad in the mountains. So if you need to, you should pull over and get a hotel. Visiting hours don't start until eight in the morning anyway."

"Visiting hours don't apply to me."

"I'll have bail money ready," she said.

"I don't know what I'd do without you," Webb said.

He could picture her reaction to his gratitude. Her top lip would snarl to the right, and both her eyes would jump up to the left behind her eyelids. She meant it to look stupid, but he thought it was adorable.

"Fuck off, Webb," Charlotte said, deflecting his gratitude. She never liked to be thanked or acknowledged for being helpful. She always said that keeping them from getting arrested or dying was enough for her.

"Fuck off, Charlotte," he said, smiling.

CHAPTER TWENTY-THREE - GLEN HOPE, PENNSYLVANIA

March 30, 2007

M rs. Davis came to a stop in front of Webb's house. Webb stiffened. His stepdad's rig was parked in the driveway. Webb didn't want to go inside, but there were witnesses waiting to see him safely home.

"Thanks for the ride, Mrs. Davis," he said, reaching for the handle.

"You're welcome, Webster. We'll see you around," she answered.

The minivan door slid itself open. Merilee reached for him, but Webb hopped out before she could take hold.

"See you at school tomorrow," he said.

He knew it wasn't enough of a goodbye, but that was all he had to give. He pushed the door, prompting it to automatically roll closed before Merilee had a chance to object.

Webb pretended he was walking around to the back of his house, but as soon as Mrs. Davis' tail lights faded around the bend, he changed his direction and started walking toward the little park next to the creek. He didn't know what he was going to do, but he figured he could kill some time until his stepdad passed out.

He approached the swing set and flopped down on a swing. A shadow moved out from under the slide.

"What are you doing here?" Bree said.

Webb froze. He wasn't expecting to run into anyone, especially not *her.* They hadn't shared a word, let alone a sentence, since he closed his front door on her.

"My stepdad's back," Webb said, trying to sound casual.

"Oh." She looked over her shoulder and then back down to her feet. "I guess this is the place to come to avoid dads."

"Huh?" His thoughts were still a little fuzzy from the weed.

"Nothing. My mom's helping set up the craft thing at church. I don't want to be alone with him."

She stepped into the light, and Webb realized she was still in her dress from the dance. The fabric hardly grazed her thigh. It was strapless, hugging just above her breasts. Webb tried to picture them underneath.

"Sorry. I thought things would be better when your mom came home."

One look at her face washed away everything she had done to hurt him in the past.

"I think it's getting worse." She turned away toward the creek. "Did you ever want to be clean? Like clean of every terrible thing you'd done or that's happened to you?"

"I don't know. Not really."

She reached her arms around her back and tugged the zipper down. Her dress fell in a puddle at her feet, leaving her there in a strapless bra and underwear. After giving him a steely look, she marched toward the creek.

"What are you doing?" he called after her.

"I'm baptizing myself," she answered and climbed down the bank to the water's edge.

"That's a really bad idea. It's freezing." He held out his hand. "Come back up. You're going to get hurt or drown," he argued, but Bree didn't listen.

She unhooked her bra and wiggled out of her underwear, naked in the moonlight until she waded into the creek. He'd never seen the water so high. Webb hoped her footing held.

"Bree, seriously. Stop!"

She ducked under the water. He held his breath too, searching the dark, rushing water for her. When she came back up with her hair slicked back, he let it go.

"I'm really fucked-up, and I'm sorry," she shouted to the sky.

He jumped into the creek, hoping he didn't get swept under. When he reached her, she was crying. Unsure of what to do, he wrapped his arms around her. She looked up at him. And without asking, or thinking too much about it, he kissed her on her mouth.

CHAPTER TWENTY-FOUR · GLEN HOPE, PENNSYLVANIA

March 31, 2007

When the doorbell rang the next morning, Webb wasn't expecting it to be her. She was dressed in black pants and a patterned shirt.

Webb stood in the doorway, scratching his ribs. He had just woken up.

"Hey," she said, pushing past him. "I'm going to work with your mom." In the context of this conversation, last night didn't happen.

"Oh right. Cool." Webb walked into the kitchen, even though he wanted to stay. His mom came down the stairs a few seconds later. They were gone before Webb's toast popped up.

He heard a groan from upstairs. It was weird to hear another deep voice in the house. These days, Gary was only home twice a month.

His stepdad plodded down the stairs.

"Hey, welcome home." Webb said it first to make it seem like he was happy to see him.

"Are you trying to look like a girl with that hair?" he asked Webb with a scowl.

Webb ran his fingers through his bangs and mumbled something about not having time to get it cut. The truth was he had asked his mom to cut it this way. Webb liked his hair a little long in the front now.

"I'll tell your mom to cut it after work tonight," his stepdad grumbled.

"Ok," Webb said.

"What are you doing today? Selling some Girl Scout cookies?"

There was no way he could stay in the house alone with his stepdad for the next eight hours.

"I'm hanging out with Cole. We have a group project." Webb hoped it wasn't obvious that he made up the lie on the spot.

Gary grabbed a beer out of the fridge and climbed back up the stairs. As soon as the bathroom door closed, Webb threw on some clothes, grabbed his guitar, and headed for the fort.

As far as Webb could tell, the two musty rooms had remained undisturbed since he was here with Bree a few weeks ago. He settled on the chair and pulled out his guitar. He'd been practicing every day, and his fingertips were hard enough that he didn't feel the cut of the strings.

He strummed out chords and started singing. The words escaped in perfect rhymes and rhythms. When he was sure he wouldn't lose the lyrics, he'd furiously scribble them on the back of his chord cheat sheet.

Something took over, feeding words and melodies in his head, moving his fingers around the neck of the guitar. It wasn't until he had to squint to read the paper that he realized it was almost dark outside. He packed up the guitar and jogged home. He needed a band. He had to call Brent and Chris.

WEBB CAUGHT a ride to Tyrone with his mom the next morning. He was hoping Bree would ride with them, but she was only assisting his mom on Saturdays until school let out.

"What are you going to do again?" his mom asked.

"Jason's cousins and I are starting a band," he said, frustrated that he had already told her twice. "What's so hard to understand?"

"Nothing. I didn't know you wanted to be in a band, that's all." She blotted her lipstick on a napkin and put the car in reverse.

"My dad was in a band with Uncle Rick," Webb reminded her. She tightened her grip on the wheel.

"Trust me, you don't want to be like them."

"Why are you so against me being in a band?"

"I'm not. As long as your grades are good and you plan on going to college, I support you."

"Why wouldn't I go to college?" Her logic was maddening. He joined a band, and suddenly he was dropping out of high school, moving to Philadelphia, not going to college, and slinking home in a year to get married. He wasn't his dad.

"You will. I didn't mean for it to come out like that." She stared out at the road for a while. "You're smart. You can be anything you want to be."

"Except a guitar player in a band."

She let out a sigh. "I want you to make good choices, that's all."

Brent and Chris' house was built into a hill, so only part of the basement was tucked underground. Webb envied their private retreat. Soda cans, chip bags, and old sandwich wrappers rested between guitars, amps, and other equipment Webb couldn't identify. Chris' drums sat against the far wall on top of a threadbare rug.

Now that he was here, he didn't know where to begin. Should he sit down and start playing his songs? That seemed weird. He didn't have to worry about what to do for long. Chris pulled out a bong and lit the bowl. Brent put on some music, and they took turns sucking long drags of smoke through the tube.

"Won't your parents smell it?" Webb asked.

"Nah. They never come down here. Our dad can't smell anything anyway. His nose is all fucked up from chemicals at work. But you might want to leave your shirt outside if your mom can smell," Chris said.

Webb shrugged off the black button-down that he wore over everything these days and draped it over the handrail next to the basement door.

When they were all stoned, Brent reached for a guitar, and Chris shuffled over to the drums. At first they played along with the music. No one spoke as they searched for melodies they could imitate.

Webb felt clumsy and stupid. He kept playing the wrong notes, or he was too slow, or he'd miss something. If Brent and Chris noticed, they didn't let him know. They were making mistakes too.

For the rest of the afternoon they fumbled through every Red Hot Chili Peppers song on *Californication*. By the time his mom pulled up, Webb didn't care if he hit a wrong note. In the rare moments when they all found the right notes together, it was bliss.

When he got in the car, he was still buzzed. Nervous he'd say something spacey to tip her off, he decided to act tired and rest his head against the passenger window.

"Did you have a good time?" she asked after a while.

"Yeah, it was cool. We sat around and played along to *Californication*," he said.

"I thought you were writing your own songs."

"I... I didn't feel like sharing them yet. It's kind of personal, you know?"

She nodded. Webb could tell she was suspicious about something. "Is there something you want to talk about?"

Webb wondered if he disclosed too much. Was that something potheads did? "Not really."

"Not even about you and Bree?"

Relief. He could talk about that.

"She's with Jason," he said.

"I know, but I was wondering if that bothers you. It seems like you like her."

"As a friend. I have a girlfriend, Mom. And this is weird."

"Bree needs good friends now. Her mom's sick."

A twinge of guilt bit at him. "What's wrong with her?"

"I forget what it's called. Something with her liver," his mom said and reached over to tousle his hair. "Don't tell her I told you."

"I won't." He batted her away and closed his eyes again, pressing harder into the window.

CHAPTER TWENTY-FIVE - GLEN HOPE, PENNSYLVANIA

April 16, 2007

It was a little past midnight when he heard the rapping on his window. He bolted upright. The air in his nose felt sharp. He was ready to scramble out of bed and run out of his room until he realized Bree was on the other side, pleading to come in.

He slowly slid the window up to minimize the screeching of worn-out wood against the cracked paint on the frame. Without a word, he helped her inside, unsure if this was a dream.

"Can I stay here?" she asked.

"Yeah, of course."

She climbed into his bed. Her cold legs rubbed against his blanket-toasted skin. He draped an arm over her and pulled her closer.

If she wasn't shaking so hard, he might have asked her why she hadn't run to Jason's house. He didn't want to know the answer. He'd rather think it was because she could talk to him—not because his house was the most convenient.

He slipped his hand under the covers and around her waist. She inched closer. He took slow, deep breaths, filling his lungs with the smell of her hair. She had changed her shampoo. Now her hair smelled musky, exotic, spicy—not sterile like Merilee's.

"Do you like me, Webb?"

He stopped himself from turning her question into a joke. She couldn't see his face; it seemed easier to be honest.

"More than I should," he whispered.

He listened as her breath became steady and soft. The rhythm tugged him back to sleep.

"Will you really run away with me someday?" she whispered. Webb wasn't sure if she was really asking it, or if he had drifted off.

"Sure."

She seemed satisfied by his answer and snuggled down into him. She pressed back into his lap. Her hips moved gently back and forth. He felt the blood rush everything awake. He moved, hoping the pressure would graze the right spot.

Suddenly, she was on top of him. Her legs straddled him.

"Do you think about me?" she asked. Her fingers wiggled around the elastic of his boxers. Her touch. Ripples of desire and agony. He feared she'd leave him there wanting more.

"All the time," he admitted.

"Do you like this?" Her thumbs grazed the taught skin of his hips.

"Yes." His breath staggered through his nostrils, staccato with anticipation.

"What do you want to do to me?"

He couldn't tell her. He was too embarrassed to repeat the endless list out loud.

"Everything," he whispered.

"Like this?" She took his hands and positioned them on her breasts.

The muscles in his hands tightened, hesitant to explore the softness. He nodded.

"What about this?" She bent down to him. Her mouth on his. She yanked his boxers down. He felt her hand nudging her underwear to the side. And with a quick downward push, her warmth wrapped around him.

His thoughts flew too fast in his head, forming into one resounding sentence: *This is happening.* Finally, she was his. Like he'd always wanted her to be. He'd begged the universe for only a fraction of this moment. As he fell into the darkness of her body, he fought to pull himself back to awareness, but there was nothing he could do but let go.

CHAPTER TWENTY-SIX - I-70, BREEZEWOOD, PENNSYLVANIA

January 23, 2016

Plows worked to spray the snow along the berms, but they couldn't keep up. Webb concentrated on staying in the tire tracks of the cars that went before him. Big, thick flakes stuck to everything and made it harder for Webb's fatigue-dried eyes to see.

He strained to see the green mile markers. The windshield looked like it was playing television static. Every tenth of a mile, he would pass someone who had given up and pulled over, but he refused to stop. He was afraid if he did, he'd never be able to continue. The driver had been right. Rear-wheel drive sucked in the snow.

With every mile that passed, Webb's eyes drooped heavier. Blinking took three times longer than usual—almost long enough for him to drive off the road. He rolled the window down, letting the side-sweeping snow pelt him awake.

As he approached Breezewood, the Camaro struggled up the hill. He stepped on the gas, experimenting with the pedal for the right amount of pressure that would propel him forward without making the wheels spin.

At the top of the hill, the front tires slid, drifting into the other lane. Webb moved the steering wheel, but the car didn't respond. He slid faster toward the guardrail and down the hill.

Helpless, he watched the piece of metal get closer to his car. How could that be the only thing protecting him from rolling down the shaved-off side of the mountain? He kept sliding, unable to correct his trajectory. Revived by fear, he turned, trying not to move the steering wheel too fast.

He summoned every trick Gary had taught him about driving in the snow. Pump the brakes. Steer gently. Stay calm. But it didn't help; he couldn't regain control. As the tires lost their grip, the car spun, skidding down the hill sideways. There was nothing he could do. He had to let go and wait for the impact.

CHAPTER TWENTY-SEVEN - GLEN HOPE, PENNSYLVANIA

April 16, 2007

"We should skip school tomorrow," Webb said, curling into her. She flinched him away and got up.

"You mean today. It's two in the morning." She reached for the light next to his bed. It clicked but didn't come on.

"The bulb is out," he lied, pulling his curtain away to let in the light from the street. His mom couldn't pay the electric bill until Friday. He watched her cross the room, collecting her clothes. Webb didn't remember how they got there.

As she slid her underwear on, he thought he saw black marks on her inner thighs. It was hard to tell if they were shadows.

"There's something on your legs," he said.

"What? Oh yeah, I bruise easily." She hopped into her jeans. Even watching her get dressed was fascinating.

"You didn't answer me. Do you want to skip school?"

"Can't. I have an English test." She pulled her shirt over her head. He searched for something that would keep her there. He craved some sort of validation.

"So what happens now that we... you know."

"Had sex? You're acting like it's a big deal," she said, twisting her hair into a bun. A weight of disappointment landed on his abdomen.

"It's a big deal to me," he said. Didn't she know how he loved her? How he cherished her? How he would never have a bigger dream than just being near her?

"It's just sex." She laughed. "What did you think was going to happen?"

"I thought you'd break up with Jason."

"Why would I do that? Do you know how many scouts show up at practice to watch him? He's probably going to get a full scholarship to Penn State and then get drafted to the NFL."

"So?" Webb asked.

"So, he's going to make a lot of money. No offense, but I don't want to live like this," she said, pointing around Webb's room. "I'm not going to be poor."

"Just because I live here doesn't mean that I'm going to be poor." The elation of losing his virginity waned. He felt stupid. No, pathetic.

"I should go home before my mom realizes I'm not there."

"Can't you stay?"

She pushed the window up. "See you tomorrow," she said and disappeared.

THE NEXT morning, Webb watched her front door. As soon as she came out, he ran across the street.

"Wait!" he called to her.

"What are you doing?"

"I need to talk to you. I love—"

She pushed against his chest so hard that he wobbled back. "Don't ever say that to me."

"But it's the truth. I don't understand what happened last night. Did I do something wrong?"

He really wanted to ask if he was so terrible at sex that she was embarrassed for him.

"It was a mistake. Can't we pretend it didn't happen?" She rushed ahead.

A mistake. The best thing that had happened to him in his entire life was a mistake.

Webb saw Jason's hands squeezing into fists as they approached.

"What's going on, Bree?" he asked, moving closer. "Where were you last night?"

"I found something else to do," Bree said, turning her head away.

He looked at Webb. "Have anything to tell me, Turner?"

"Dude. What's your problem?" Webb asked.

"I don't know, something feels off. You look guilty," Jason said.

"Maybe the steroids are making you hallucinate," Webb said as the bus pulled up.

"Fuck you, Turner. You're a shithead, you know that?"

"I just want you to say you're sorry, Jason. You're so stupid sometimes!" Bree yelled, climbing the steps.

"I'm sorry I blew you off last night. I'll make it up to you." Jason and Bree continued to bicker all the way to the back seat.

Webb usually sat across from them, but he decided to sit two seats away—it felt safer.

For the next two stops he tried to ignore the growing realization that Bree had slept with him to get back at Jason. He wanted to ask Jason if he had put the bruises on her legs, but he couldn't do that without admitting he'd seen them. He wanted to ask Bree if last night had meant anything to her.

"I don't have to tell you anything. I know you drove Tori home from your 'guy's night' at Pizza King."

"Just tell me where you were last night," Jason said.

Webb turned back to them. "Will you leave her alone?"

"You'd like that, wouldn't you? I see the way you look at her," Jason said. "I know you've had a hard-on for her since forever."

Webb sat back down and held his middle finger over the back of his seat.

A fist clamped over his extended finger before he could retract his hand. Jason bent it back, saliva squirting out from between his clenched teeth. A crowd gathered around them to watch, but no one tried to stop Jason.

Webb scrambled up so he was facing him. His free arm flailed as he tried to grab any loose piece of clothing or skin. Jason twisted Webb's middle finger harder. Webb threw a punch, but it caught the seat. Bree pulled at Jason's shirt. With a quick swing, he pushed her off easily.

"Stop it, Jason!" she yelled.

"You think I don't know what he's trying to do?" Jason growled and yanked Webb's finger back even harder. "Didn't you hear me? He's had a hard-on for you since you moved here."

"Stop it!" Bree shrieked.

Webb heard ripping and a sickening snap. He cried out. His finger dangled.

The driver pulled the bus to the side of the road and waddled back to Webb and Jason. She wedged herself between them to break up the fight. Pain occupied every neuron firing in Webb's head. He wanted to cry or to shrink into a ball and shake with tears, but he had to suppress the agony until he was alone.

"Get to the front of the bus, both of you," she ordered.

"I think there's something wrong with my finger," Webb said, holding it up for her to see.

She staggered back, offended by the black pools of blood coagulating beneath his skin. She rushed back to her seat and called dispatch.

"Bus seven. I'm going to need emergency services…"

The back of Webb's mouth tingled with metallic saliva. As it collected near his throat, he tried not to swallow it. If he did, all the terrible things about himself would be trapped inside. It also might make him throw up. The driver ushered them outside and set flares around the perimeter of the parked bus.

"Dude, your finger is so nasty," he heard a freshman say out the window. Almost the entire bus was crowded on one side, waiting to see what would happen next.

"Do you think he's going to lose it?" someone else asked.

"Could everybody shut the fuck up?" Webb yelled. The bus driver whipped her head around and pulled out her yellow note pad. She scribbled furiously.

"That's another infraction," she said.

"You have to be kidding me," Webb said, cradling his finger into his chest. It was starting to swell, which made it hurt even more. They were twenty minutes away from school. It would take just as long to get to the hospital. It took forever to get anywhere important.

CHAPTER TWENTY-EIGHT - GLENDALE MEDICAL CENTER, COALPORT, PENNSYLVANIA

April 16, 2007

Webb's finger throbbed with more blood. It didn't look as limp since it had almost doubled in size. He wished he got a good punch in before the bus driver broke up the fight. Now Jason could relish the victory of escaping without a scratch *and* breaking Webb's finger.

The pain didn't bother him as much as the setback of his injury. How could he play guitar with a broken finger? Would it heal all weird and jagged?

After Dr. Crane shrouded his finger in a splint, Webb's mom drove him home. He tried to catch something solid from the scenery racing alongside the window, but he couldn't focus on anything. Trees, still stripped from winter, a trailer, siding peeling back and insulation puffing out, an old pickup "for sale by owner." Webb's past, present, and inevitable future.

"It seems out of character for you to fight with anyone, but I thought Jason was your best friend," she said.

"I didn't fight with him. He attacked me," Webb said. "And we're not really friends anymore."

"If you're having a hard time here, you can stay with your dad for a while."

"You're kidding, right? I'd rather be a punching bag for Jason than my dad." He said it out loud. Usually, it was better to pretend that Webb didn't have a father. But if they ever forgot, the scar on the back of his head (where his hair would never grow right) could remind them.

"Maybe it would be different now."

"The only way anything will be different is if I move away and never come back."

She frowned, not taking her eyes from the road. "Running away doesn't solve anything." She sounded like his grandma.

"But you just told me to go stay with my dad!" Webb yelled, pointing out the contradiction. He was sick of her telling him what to do when she couldn't take her own advice.

"Living with your dad isn't the same as leaving and never coming back."

"Unless you're Zoe." It was a low blow. He knew it would hurt her, but he said it anyway.

"Sometimes saying goodbye is the only way to love someone."

CHAPTER TWENTY-NINE - I-70, BREEZEWOOD, PENNSYLVANIA

January 23, 2016

The rear bumper crunched against the guardrail. The impact spun the car around. It was all happening so fast. Webb saw the white road and the darkness taking turns in his vision. He spun all the way to the traffic light at the bottom of the hill. The car jumped over a curb and came to a stop fifty yards away from the intersection.

"This is Andy from OnStar. I see that you've been in an accident. Are there any injuries?"

Webb's pulse pounded. "I don't think so," he said.

"I'm glad to hear that. Do you need emergency assistance?"

Webb looked down at his body to make sure he wasn't hurt without knowing it. "No, I'm just a little freaked out."

"If you realize something's not right, or if you need anything, press the OnStar button."

"Thanks," Webb said.

As soon as Andy clicked off, Webb's hands started shaking. He was too tired to drive. The roads were too bad.

He steered his car into the parking lot of the Holiday Inn Express. A feeling of relief settled over him when he turned off the engine.

THE LAYER of dried sweat, still on his skin from the show, itched. Even though he didn't have a change of clothes, he took a shower. The water scalded his skin pink. It felt good to be hot, clean, and not moving. He wished he had his sleeping pills. He tried to call his mom again. Still no answer.

As the wind battered against the hotel window, he thought about calling Charlotte. He wanted to talk to her and let her know he was getting a room. Instead he fell into the bed, not even needing the pills.

HE'D FORGOTTEN to close the blackout curtains. The reflection of the rising sun on the snow outside seared him awake. He examined his clothes in a pile on the bathroom floor. They seemed too dirty to put back on. Maybe he should buy new clothes before seeing her.

He was stalling.

"You are going to see her," he told himself. "It doesn't matter what you're wearing. You're not wasting any more time. You are going to see her, you fucking coward."

Webb pulled on his jeans and shirt, threw some money down for housekeeping, and walked out to the car. The plow was starting to clear out the parking lot. As Webb pulled out of the parking space, the tires spun and swerved. He got the Camaro out just before it was buried behind a wall of hard snow.

He pulled into the gas station next to the hotel. He picked up a pair of sunglasses, filled the tank, and continued north.

CHAPTER THIRTY - GLEN HOPE, PENNSYLVANIA

April 16, 2007

Merilee came over after school, frantic, half concerned about Webb's finger and half concerned about the gossip. He could break up with her right then. It would be easy to admit how he felt about Bree, that no other girl could ever approach her place of female perfection. If he was a nice guy, he wouldn't keep leading Merilee on. Wouldn't keep letting her suck him into a black hole of trivial conversation.

He pulled her into a hug and kissed the top of her head. "Don't listen to them," he said. "They want something to talk about, and this week it's me."

"But why would Jason attack you for no reason?"

"I don't know. I'm pretty sure he's on steroids. They make you crazy, you know."

Merilee's face washed over with understanding. "That makes total sense. He flipped out on my brother a few weeks ago because he took too long to go after a light turned green."

"Yep. Sounds like steroids." Webb shrugged and changed the subject. "We should do something fun this weekend."

Merilee perked up. He had never instigated plans in the past, but Webb felt generous in the haze of his guilt.

"I guess bowling is out," she said, gently stroking his hand, careful not to touch his finger.

"We could see a movie, though. What about *Disturbia*?"

She wrinkled her nose. "Too scary. Oh! What about the new Will Ferrell movie about ice skating?"

"Sure."

"I have to get home for dinner," she hinted.

The painkillers made Webb's thoughts fire slower than usual, so it took him a few seconds to realize she wanted him to walk her home. He reached for her hand, and she accepted, but the contact of their skin still felt empty.

Webb didn't know how to regain her trust; after all, he was guilty. No matter how much he wanted things to be simple, he loved Bree and would never look at Merilee the way she wanted him to.

They concentrated on the silence between their steps. While Webb hoped the silence would continue, he could see Merilee scrambling in her head to put her hesitation into words. *Please don't make me talk about this*, Webb thought as they turned down her street.

The light above the garage was on. They came to a stop underneath it.

"You're sure you don't like her like that?" she asked.

Webb wanted to look away, so she couldn't see the lies forming, but he kept his gaze directed at her eyes. He softened his face, except for his forehead; he kept it wrinkled with sincerity. He wasn't sure why he kept clinging to this relationship. If he told her the truth, he could end it now and wait for Bree to finally want him back. That's what was supposed to happen.

"*You* are my girlfriend. I only like one girl like that," he said. Although they were separate true statements, Webb knew she would string them together to form what she wanted to hear.

His expression, the appeal in his voice, or maybe Merilee's hope allowed her to believe him. Webb knew that she didn't want to hear how Bree had curled in bed with him or how she'd claimed Webb's virginity. Merilee wanted to hear that she herself was the only one and that Webb loved her.

Merilee collected her puffy curls and twisted them next to her neck. She stared at him. He knew she wanted him to kiss her. He knew that was what he was supposed to do, but she was always so needy. He didn't want to train her like Pavlov's dog to expect a kiss every time she felt inadequate.

"See you tomorrow," he said and turned to walk back home.

Dusk settled in as Webb treaded on the shoulder of the road toward his house. He wished Bree would appear, as she had a tendency to do. Maybe he'd see her wandering down the side of the road or running out of the park. He fantasized about giving her the kiss Merilee wanted so badly.

He thought about crossing the street to the park. Webb pictured Bree there on a swing, slowly rocking back and forth, wishing that he would happen to go there. As he passed Jason's house, he thought of going right to Bree's door and telling her how he felt—that he couldn't keep living like this. That she had to change her mind.

Webb was deep in an imaginary struggle with Bree that he didn't see Jason jump out of the shadows. Jason's arms hooked around Webb's throat, locking down his windpipe. His grip was so tight that Webb couldn't wheeze a breath in or out. The short breath he took right before the impact struggled to get out.

With his good hand, he reached up to pry Jason's forearm away, but it was bigger than two of Webb's biceps. Webb kicked and squirmed. Jabbing his elbow back, he tried to get a few good hits in, but Jason didn't budge.

Webb wanted to cough. He could feel his face turning dark red with blood that begged for oxygen. His ears picked up a low ring that rolled like the fading echo of a tornado siren. It was getting harder to fight back.

"She told me everything," Jason finally hissed in his ear. "I saw what you did to her."

Webb wiggled some more, trying to find a weak place in Jason's grip. If he could have choked out words, he would have. He could feel his muscles slackening, and the field of his vision grew soft and dark around the edges. With the last of his strength, Webb reached back and jabbed Jason's eye sockets, pressing his fingers in them as hard as he could.

Jason's hands darted to his eyes, and Webb fell to the ground. The flow of air stung his throat and lungs as it poured in.

"What the fuck, dude?" Jason yelled, cupping his eyes with his hands. "Your nails scratched my eyeball."

"You were choking me," Webb said.

They both collapsed on Jason's lawn. Jason wiped the stream of water from his face and Webb held his bruised throat. They'd had scrappy fights in elementary school, the worst one after Webb threw Jason's Austin-Healey Hot Wheel into the rain gutter above his porch, but this one was different. There was a rage behind it that Webb had never seen.

Afraid of what Jason might do next, he scrambled to his feet and ran home.

CHAPTER THIRTY-ONE - GLEN HOPE, PENNSYLVANIA

April 17, 2007

When he got to the bus stop, Bree was already there. He wondered if he should tell her what a juiced-up psycho Jason was. He wondered if Jason had told her anything.

"Oh my gosh," Bree cried when she saw his face. "When did that happen?"

A yellow-and-blue bruise collared Webb's throat. He had managed to get a more noticeable black eye in the struggle. He shrugged. He wanted her to feel sorry for him.

"Jason jumped me on my way home from Merilee's last night," Webb said. "What did you tell him?"

Bree rubbed her face, pressing her palms into her eyes.

"What did you tell him?" Webb said again.

"I told him…" She looked around for an escape. "I told him that you kind of forced yourself on me."

"What?" Webb yelled so loud that his question bounced down the street, off houses, off the mountain a few miles away, and then back to them.

"I panicked."

"You have to tell him it's not true! I could go to jail. Seriously."

She flapped her hands in front of her body, like she did when she felt helpless. "I know. I'm so sorry," she cried.

"You have to fix it. Tell him it's not true. Fuck, Bree. That's... fuck."

Webb almost turned in to go back home. How was he supposed to go to school? He couldn't walk down the halls with everyone thinking that he had forced himself on Bree.

"I can't tell him," she said. She turned away and ran back to her house as the bus approached.

"You're just going to run away?" he called after her. "You have to tell him it's not true!"

WEBB DIDN'T know how bad it would be. He thought maybe the accusation was isolated between the three of them, but when he got on the bus his classmates wouldn't look at him. They all turned away as he walked past, in a weird, teenage, group-think choreography that almost looked like they'd rehearsed it before he got on.

He sat in his seat, wishing Bree were there to defend his innocence. He hoped Merilee would decide to ride the bus today instead of driving with Pete, but when they pulled up to Merilee's stop, she wasn't there.

The forty-five-minute ride seemed three times longer than usual. Webb resorted to reading his history book, but he read the same paragraph over and over as the news spread and the taunting grew louder.

The girl behind him said, "I heard Bree's parents are selling their house and moving to Altoona to get away from him. That's probably why she's not on the bus."

Webb snapped the book shut and stood. "I can hear you all, and it's not true." He plopped back down in his seat.

"That's what a rapist would say," a high-pitched voice called out from the back of the bus.

The whispers and lack of eye contact continued when he got to school. He went straight to Merilee's locker and waited there for her. She would believe him. He craned his neck as he caught a glimpse of her through the crowd.

A huddle of girls, the same girls from the dance, surrounded her in a comforting circle. Merilee didn't see Webb at first, but then, for a second, their eyes locked. She quickly covered her face with a tissue and leaned back into the circle.

Webb settled into first period, keeping his head down, wishing he could go home sick. After attendance, the class phone rang. Mr. Pratt placed it back in the cradle, and called out to Webb. "Mr. Turner, you're wanted in the office."

Webb let his head fall back with the fatigue of what was happening. In less than twenty-four hours, his finger was broken, he had almost been choked to death, he lost his girlfriend, and he was accused of raping his dream girl.

Then he got scared. What if the police were waiting for him? What if he was going to get pulled into a room and interrogated? Why couldn't Bree be here to tell them the truth?

He walked into the office, scanning for police uniforms, but the office looked like it did on any other day. He gave his pass to the secretary and sat in a chair, waiting to be called into the principal's office.

"Mr. Turner?" Principal Wake said. "You can come in now."

He stopped in the door when he saw the school psychologist, Mrs. Denny.

"What's going on?" Webb asked, picking at the tape around his splint.

"Webster, we've heard some things circulating around school. A few of your classmates have expressed concern, and I wanted to check with you... to get your side of the story," Mrs. Denny said.

"Bree made it up, I swear," Webb said.

Principal Wake shot a questioning glance at Mrs. Denny. "No one said anything about Bree..."

"We're concerned by your fight with Jason yesterday, because he broke your finger. I wanted to make sure you knew you could come to me for support. Are you being bullied?" Mrs. Denny asked.

Webb sat for a moment. He could tell Mrs. Denny that Jason was bullying him. Jason would probably be suspended from the baseball team for the rest of the season and maybe even get kicked off the football team next year. Part of him wanted to make that happen—to destroy Jason's dreams too. The scouts wouldn't come. He wouldn't get a scholarship to Penn State. But no matter how much he wanted to ruin Jason's escape from Glen Hope, he couldn't.

"No, it was a misunderstanding," Webb said. "Can I go to the nurse, though? I feel dizzy."

CHAPTER THIRTY-TWO - I-99, OUTSIDE BEDFORD, PENNSYLVANIA

January 23, 2016

In less than an hour, he'd arrive in Altoona. Now that the miles were shrinking, Webb panicked when he thought about what she would look like. Would she be conscious? Would she want to see him?

The phone rang in the car.

"Hey, Char," he said before she had a chance to speak.

"How was it?"

"I'm still driving. I had to get a hotel last night. There was an accident." He paused, wishing he hadn't let that slip. "I'm an hour away, though."

Silence on the other end of the line.

"Charlotte?" Webb asked, wondering if the call was dropped. He was getting into the less populated areas where cell service suffered from the same lack of resources as the people living in the tiny houses.

"I'm here. I... never mind. Is it snowing?" She sounded exhausted. Webb hoped she hadn't stayed up all night worrying about him.

"It's stopped for now, but there's a lot on the roads." He couldn't believe they were talking about weather. Charlotte was acting weird.

"Where are you guys now?"

"The bus is stuck in D.C. They might not be able to get it out until tonight. Do you want me to get you on a flight out of State College tomorrow?"

Webb hadn't thought that far out. If he made it to Bree in time, would he be able to leave her? If he didn't, would he be able to play?

"It's fine if you can't. Vince can fill in. Not a big deal... By the way, I arranged for your phone to be delivered to the hospital."

"I don't say it enough, but you are pretty amazing. I know you're going to say 'fuck off,' but it's true," he said.

She chuckled. "Actually, I was going to say, 'thank you' and *then* 'fuck off.'"

"I'm glad you decided to change it up."

"Let me know when you get there, and I'll send your phone."

"Fuck off, Charlotte," Webb sang.

"Fuck off, Webb," she answered. He heard her let out a short laugh before she disconnected.

Webb had the road to himself. The closer he got, the faster he pushed the car. He didn't notice he was speeding until he saw the flashing lights. Fuck. He eased the car to the shoulder.

The cop took his time walking from the squad car to the Camaro. While he waited, Webb pulled out the packet of identification papers from the glove compartment and fished his ID from his wallet. He'd never been pulled over before.

Webb rolled down the window and handed everything over before the cop had a chance to ask.

"Webster Turner?" the cop asked, surprised.

A fan. Maybe he'd let him off.

"Yeah," Webb said, flipping up his sunglasses to show his eyes.

"I'm going to have to ask you to step out of the car," the cop said.

"If I could just have my ticket, I'll pay it and go. It's kind of an emergency..." Webb pleaded. He didn't have time for selfies or autographs.

"There's a warrant out for your arrest," the cop explained. "I'm going to have to ask you to step out of the vehicle."

"What? I think you have the wrong Webster Turner."

"Please don't make me ask you again. Now, step out of the automobile."

Webb unbuckled his seatbelt and opened the car door. Warrant? For what? He didn't have any parking tickets, unless they were from years ago.

"Up against the vehicle please, hands on the roof, feet spread," the officer instructed. Webb couldn't believe this was happening to him. The officer ran his hands down Webb's legs, patting him down for weapons.

"Is this really necessary?" Webb asked. He couldn't go to the police station. Pulling over to sleep last night had already cost him too much time. He estimated how much cash he had in his wallet. Fifty bucks was an embarrassing bribe. It would probably get him arrested.

"Turn around, keep your hands in the air."

Webb obeyed.

"Now give me a hug, you piece of shit."

CHAPTER THIRTY-THREE - GLENDALE HIGH SCHOOL, FLINTON, PENNSYLVANIA

April 17, 2007

Webb waited for his mom to pick him up at school. He'd quoted as many concussion symptoms as he could remember. It worked.

He knew he couldn't stay home for the rest of the school year, but maybe if he could persuade Bree to stick up for him or to somehow publicly declare that she'd made it up, he'd be able to finish out the year.

But Webb's mom didn't pick him up; his stepdad did.

"You know what's bullshit? I'm meeting Randy at the lake in an hour, but I have to drive your faggot ass home first," his stepdad said when they got into the car.

Webb couldn't decide if it would have been better to stay at school.

"And what's this bullshit about you getting in a fight on the bus and not even taking a swing? I didn't raise you to be a wuss," Gary continued. "Now I have to pick up my pussy faggot of a stepson because he got what he deserved."

He held his mouth with his good hand and pinched his lips closed so hard, he could feel them turning white. If he said anything, it would only invite the inevitable sooner. At least if they made it home, he might be able to outrun his stepdad and hide until he passed out for the night.

"You forget how to talk, or are you admitting that you're out there sucking dicks? I mean, look at your hair and your clothes." He reached over and grabbed a handful of Webb's bangs, which were long enough to cover his forehead. His stepdad pulled until Webb's eyes watered and the weakest strands from the clump ripped out from their roots.

"Please, Gary," Webb cried, immediately regretting it.

He was supposed to call him "Dad."

Webb's head knocked off the window, thumping dull pain down his neck into his chest. The impact snaked its way to his finger.

His stepdad took another handful of hair and shoved it into the window again.

"I'm glad you're not my kid. If you were, you'd dress right and like girls like you're supposed to."

"I do like girls," Webb said into the window, curling his body around the seat belt.

Webb didn't know why he said it. Gary wasn't asking. He didn't want to hear Webb's response, didn't want to know Webb existed.

He felt like he was ten again. Scared, small, powerless. He imagined punching back and not stopping until someone pulled his bloody hands away.

CHAPTER THIRTY-FOUR - I-99, OUTSIDE BEDFORD, PENNSYLVANIA

January 23, 2016

Webb looked closer at the uniformed officer and read the name on his badge: "Robinson."

"Jason?" Webb asked.

"What's up, shithead?" Jason confirmed and pulled Webb into a hug.

"You're a cop?"

"I'm not a male stripper, if that's what you're wondering." Jason grabbed a handful of his stomach and shook it. "This is crazy. Hailey and I were just talking about you."

"You still talk to her?"

"I have to. We have three kids."

"Shit. That's... wow."

"Yeah, I knocked her up right before I left for training camp. I guess it all worked out. I didn't make the cut, but look at you! You fucking did it, man."

Webb felt more uncomfortable talking about his fame with Jason than with strangers. Maybe it was because Webb knew Jason could see through the facade. It would be easy for him to confirm that Webb was just a white-trash kid from a forgettable town in the middle of nowhere who'd tricked the universe into letting him escape.

"I got lucky," Webb said with a shrug.

"You worked for it. Don't be such a modest shithead."

"Do you talk to anyone else from high school?" Webb asked, changing the subject.

"Merilee's a teacher. Our oldest had her last year. They moved out to Tyrone because Cole is in charge of some computer bullshit at AccuWeather. She's due any day."

For some reason it stung. Merilee was married and on the trajectory to drive her own kids to dances in a minivan. The world he'd left behind had matured and evolved. It didn't seem to care if he came along or not.

"It's good to see you," Webb mused.

"Yeah, we all thought you'd come home after a year, but you did it. You fucking did it, dude."

Webb stood there awkwardly, still not sure if Jason was going to give him a ticket.

"We're playing in Philly tomorrow. I can get you tickets if you want to go…" Webb offered.

"Is that a bribe?"

"Don't be such a shithead," Webb answered and gave him a friendly punch on the shoulder. "I probably won't be there anyway, but if you wanted to go and hang out with Brent and Chris backstage…"

"What do you mean you won't be there?"

"I'm going home to see Bree."

"That girl invented a whole new level of alcoholism." Jason saw the hurt look on Webb's face and changed his voice to a more suitable, sober tone. "She's been on the prayer list at church for a while. I saw her a few weeks ago. Didn't recognize her."

Webb looked at the side of the road, watching the cars spray melted snow from their tires. Somehow, hearing the details from his mom wasn't as painful as hearing them from Jason.

"My mom said they don't think she's going to make it much longer. She might already be gone," Webb said. The last two words struggled to find their way out.

"Sorry, dude. She was, is, a cool girl."

"Yeah." He changed the subject. "So, do you want me to tell my manager to leave four tickets for you at will call?"

"Nah, I have to work. You should get out of here."

"Thanks, man. It was good to see you, really." Webb reached for the car door. "Tell your mom I said hi."

"I will. And be careful; you're missing a tail light," Jason added before heading back to his cruiser.

Webb turned the ignition and merged back onto the highway. There were signs for Altoona. He was close.

CHAPTER THIRTY-FIVE - GLEN HOPE, PENNSYLVANIA

April 17, 2007

 Gary dropped him off at home. As soon as the car was out of sight, Webb ran across the street. He banged on Bree's door and rang the doorbell. Mrs. Brewer answered.

"What happened to your face?"

"Nothing." He touched his bruised eye. "Is Bree home?"

"She's still at school," Mrs. Brewer said, like Webb was either stupid or unstable.

Webb knew she wasn't in school. She hadn't gotten on the bus. And even though he wanted her to know how it felt to be betrayed, he pretended he didn't realize it was still early.

"Oh, right. I stayed home today. I'll come over after school," he said.

Where else would she be? Jason was suspended for the week. She could be with him somewhere, but Webb doubted his mom would let him have visitors.

Jason might have snuck her into his room, but that seemed unlikely. Before he gave up, Webb decided to check the fort. Just in case.

He ran all the way, even though it made his head pound with pain where it had connected with the window.

He approached the fort cautiously at first. He wanted to make sure Jason wasn't in there too. He listened outside for a few seconds before sneaking closer. He grew braver with every step. By the time he reached the door, he was convinced that the fort was empty. There wasn't any movement or sound coming from inside, but the plywood door was slightly ajar.

Webb pulled it open. He saw her splayed feet first. The rest of her body lay in the smaller room.

"Bree?" Webb asked, pushing down the building alarm in his chest.

She didn't answer.

"Hey, wake up," he said a little louder and bent down to shake her foot. She didn't move.

He ducked into the smaller room and pulled her head up. It flopped to the side without the support of his hand.

"Bree?" He said it louder.

He didn't know what to do.

"What happened? Did you take something? What did you take?" He shook her and leaned over her face. Her eyes were open, but she stared past him like he was invisible. He thought he felt a soft flutter of breath stream out of her nose. Then again, it could be his own heavy breath reflecting off her face back to him.

Webb slipped his hand down her shirt. The skin of her chest felt cold and damp. He thought he could feel her heart beating, but it may have been his own racing pulse pumping in his fingertips.

As the panic built, he darted his eyes up and down her body. He didn't see any blood. Her purse dangled from the back of the lawn chair.

It felt like an invasion of privacy, but he dug through it anyway. He didn't find a note. Just make-up, a collapsible brush, and a plastic baggie coated with a white, powdery residue. He shoved the baggie into his pocket and picked her up.

He carried her like his mom used to carry him out of the car after he fell asleep on the way home from the salon's Christmas party. He didn't know how he was going to make it down the uneven path back to the road, so he didn't think about it. Instead, he concentrated on each individual step.

At first he was surprised by his own strength. Aside from the pounding pain in his broken finger and bruised temple, supporting Bree in his arms was easy. He wanted to stop and see if she was breathing, but he knew time was his enemy. Whatever pumped through her blood was slowly stealing her from him.

Maybe he should talk to her. He'd seen that in movies where someone would beg an overdosed friend to listen. They'd say *"stay with me,"* but Webb felt stupid when he said it out loud. He trudged forward in silence and scrambled to form a plan.

He'd get to the road and flag down a car, if there was a car. Otherwise, he'd have to carry her all the way home. Her mom would know what to do.

His ankles wobbled on the rocks that jutted up from the path. His grip on Bree slipped. He hefted her body, renegotiating his arms. They were starting to shake with fatigue. He kept going. He was almost to the road.

When he got to the fence, he curled his body around her and ducked through the rusted barbs. The ends raked his back as he forced his way to the other side. The shaking from his arms spread to his torso. He hoped there was a car driving by when he made it to the road.

"We're almost there," he whispered to her. "Don't let go. Stay with me."

The ground was soft on this side of the fence, and with the added weight, Webb struggled against the mud that kept grabbing his steps. Each step forward took twice the effort. He could finally see the road. It was empty, but any second a car might drive by. His grip slipped again. He'd be lucky to make it to the road carrying her.

He didn't want to let her go, but if he left her in the grass, he could run and flag down a car. That's what he had to do.

As gently and quickly as he could, he eased Bree's body to the ground. The absence of her weight made his arms feel like they were floating up— like someone had tied two giant helium balloons to his wrists. Without a glance back, Webb took off for the road.

About half a mile away, he saw the glare of the sun reflecting off a windshield. He ran into the middle of the road, waving his arms, shouting.

As the vehicle approached, it slowed. Webb recognized the blue minivan. Merilee's brother Pete rolled down his window.

"What are you doing, Dick-shinary?"

"Bree took something. I don't know if she's breathing." Saying it stirred his emotions into a slurry of guilt, fear, panic, and sadness. Tears waited in the edges of his ducts, ready to expose him if he wasn't careful.

"What did you do to her?" Pete demanded, getting out of the car. Webb couldn't tell if he was going to hit him or help him.

"Nothing! I didn't do anything, I swear," Webb said. "She made up a story. She didn't go to school. I went looking for her—"

"Where is she?" Pete's friend Nick said as he came around from the passenger side.

Pete and Nick ran to keep up with Webb as they followed him into the grass. Webb led them to where he had left her. Lying stone-still on the ground, she looked dead. Her lips looked like they were outlined with a blue ballpoint pen.

"Why didn't you call 911?" Pete asked as he scooped Bree up. He was over six feet tall, and Bree looked like a child in his arms.

"I don't have a cell phone," Webb said, his voice getting higher.

"This is not how I wanted to spend Senior Skip Day," Nick said, flipping open his phone.

Suddenly, Webb wanted to be the one holding her, even if his arms couldn't support her weight for long. He wanted to be close to her, to will her to live. But there was a relief in letting her go. He had done what he could. He had found her and got her this far.

The dispatcher told Nick to take her to Glendale Medical Center in Coalport. It would be faster to go right there than to wait for an ambulance. They would be ready for her. Webb felt every second pass like someone was sucking the breath out of his lungs.

They were less than five minutes away when a guttural noise rattled out from deep in her throat. Webb turned her head so it faced him.

"I think she's dying. Can't you go any faster?"

Pete stepped harder on the gas. The engine struggled to respond, but Pete didn't give up. He kept his foot on the pedal and took the turns in the road too fast. Webb held on to the door with one hand and Bree with the other.

CHAPTER THIRTY-SIX - GLENDALE MEDICAL CENTER, COALPORT, PENNSYLVANIA

April 17, 2007

Mrs. Brewer was right behind them when they pulled into the parking lot. Nick had called her after he hung up with 911. The medical staff raced out, hooking Bree up to oxygen and electrodes. A nurse approached Webb.

"Do you know what she took?'

"No. I wasn't with her, but I found this in her purse." He pulled out the plastic bag and handed it to her.

"Do you know if she ever took illegal drugs?" the nurse asked Webb.

"No," Webb said. The nurse turned to Bree's mom.

"Do you have any prescription pills in your home that she could have gotten a hold of?"

Bree's mom started listing pill after pill that either she or Mr. Brewer took. Webb didn't recognize any of the names, but most of them ended in "cet."

"We'll do what we can," the nurse assured her and followed the gurney inside.

Bree's mom released them from the waiting room, thanking Nick and Pete again and again, but she didn't thank Webb. In fact, she went out of her way to look at everyone but him.

Nick and Pete started to leave, but Webb stayed. He had to find out if Bree would be ok.

"Webster, aren't you going to go with them?" Mrs. Brewer asked.

"No, I'll stay here," he said, making it clear that he wasn't asking for permission.

It was a waiting room; he could be there if he wanted to.

"I think it would be better if you left," she said.

"Why?"

"Because this is none of your business."

"I found her. She's alive because I carried her out of the woods and flagged down a car."

His temples pounded with rage. He felt his face take on his stepdad's expressions. The last hour had added twenty years to his confidence.

He pointed his finger at Mrs. Brewer. "It's *your* fault she's here. So I don't care if you think I should go."

The room around him seemed blurry. The only thing in focus was Mrs. Brewer's look of shock. It was different from Bree's shocked face, less hurt and more entitled.

Mrs. Brewer stood speechless for a moment and then reached for Webb and hugged him. She wailed into his shoulder, which didn't seem strong enough to catch her grief, but Webb stood still and let her. It felt better than standing there alone.

When the nurse came out, she motioned for Mrs. Brewer to come. Webb strained to hear. He heard clips of the conversation, words like "stable," "just in time," "three months along," and "abuse."

Webb's eyes darted from the nurse to Mrs. Brewer. Abuse? He thought about the bruises.

She shuffled back, staring past everything like she was trying to see through a two-way mirror.

"Please go home, Webster," she said.

He shook his head.

"Get out of here!" Mrs. Brewer screamed.

Webb stood in front of her, mute.

"Go! This is none of your business!"

He didn't have the strength to stand up to her again. At least he knew Bree was stable and would live. He'd found her just in time. The nurse confirmed it.

He walked to Pizza King and called his mom for a ride home. He scrounged in his pockets. He had enough change to buy a soda, which the girl at the counter refilled four times before his mom picked him up.

When he got in the car, he told his mom almost everything. About the accusations, about the fort, about Bree sneaking into his window. He told her about the bruises (although not exactly where they were).

"What did the nurse mean by 'signs of abuse'?" Webb asked.

His mom grew quiet and looked at him from the corner of her eye.

"I don't know. There are different kinds, physical, maybe sexual…" she said. The word made them both uncomfortable.

"I didn't do anything to her, Mom."

"I know. I believe you."

He sat at his window for the rest of the day into the night, waiting for Mrs. Brewer's headlights to turn down the street and into the driveway. Around ten o'clock, they did. Webb strained to see if Bree got out of the car, but Mrs. Brewer got out alone.

CHAPTER THIRTY-SEVEN - GLEN HOPE, PENNSYLVANIA

April 17, 2007

Webb's mom went across the street as soon as his stepdad passed out. Webb wanted to go and hide in the shadows of the Brewers' wraparound porch. He wanted to hear everything first-hand, uncensored, but he stayed behind.

"This is between mothers," his mom said before she left.

He perched on his windowsill with a pair of old plastic binoculars. It was too dark to see anything through the cheap lenses. He cracked his window, hoping some of the conversation would drift across the street and into his room, but Mrs. Brewer invited his mom in, destroying that plan too.

Webb was left to stare at the Brewers' closed front door for ten minutes before it swung open again, casting a beam of light back to Webb's house. He took the stairs two at a time.

"Bree is conscious. They are pretty sure she will make a full recovery. Mrs. Brewer is very sorry for how she treated you," Webb's mom said when she walked inside.

"Why was she so mad?" Webb asked.

"You are not to repeat this, do you understand?"

Webb nodded.

"Bree was three months pregnant," his mom said.

A sourness bubbled in Webb's stomach as he quickly did the math. The baby couldn't be his, or Jason's.

"Are you sure she was, you know?" He didn't feel old enough to repeat the word "pregnant." It had to be a mistake.

His mom steeled her eyes. "Yes, and Mrs. Brewer is grateful that you saved Bree."

Her face shifted and her chin dimpled, shaking. She reached for Webb, pulling him close, holding him into her chest. Usually, he would resist or keep his arms straight at his sides until she released him, but not today. He wound his arms over hers and squeezed back. They were almost the same height, he thought, but Webb was finally taller.

HE STAYED home from school the next day. He had to see her, to make sure she really came home.

His stepdad woke up just before noon. When Webb heard Gary stir, he slipped outside. He didn't have a destination in mind; he just started walking.

Since yesterday, his finger ached. It was a deep pain that pumped heat with each heartbeat. It was better if he kept his hand above his heart, but that looked stupid. He crossed his arm over his chest and rested his hand on his collarbone. The throbbing lessened, but the pain was still there.

Webb ambled along the side of the road, kicking through the tiny black cinders that were leftover from the winter. He kicked his way to Jason's house. Webb knew he was home. He felt like he should talk to him. It was probably a terrible idea, but maybe he would know who Bree was with and find out who got her pregnant.

As he walked up the drive, he thought of a way to bring it up without revealing the secret. Jason came out to his porch before Webb started up the steps.

"What do you want, Turner?" he asked.

"I'm not here to fight with you."

"You should have thought of that before you took advantage of my girlfriend."

Jason looked like he was ready to unleash a windmill of punches again, so Webb backed up a few steps.

"Come on. You know that's not true. Think about it. You know me, Jason," Webb said.

Jason looked away. Webb sensed that Jason wanted to blame him for something, or to get back at him for living across the street from Bree, or being invited into the glow of her charisma.

"You told the whole school that I raped her. That's pretty fucked-up," Webb said.

"Bree said you forced yourself on her. I saw the bruises," Jason said. His words sounded unsure now, like he was seriously comparing the evidence of their friendship against Bree's claim.

"Dude, she tried to kill herself yesterday. She has problems," Webb said.

"You're a fucking liar, Turner. She'd never do that."

Webb realized he didn't know. Why would he? He was grounded for getting suspended. No calls, no socialization.

"Call her house. She took a bunch of her mom's pain pills. I found her in the fort. Nick and Pete helped take her to Glendale." Webb hated recounting the story, saying it out loud, making her sound unstable.

"I don't believe you," Jason said, turning to go back inside.

"I don't care if you believe me. I wanted to see if you've noticed anything weird about her lately."

"No. She's the same as she always is," Jason said. He shot a nervous look back into the house. "I should go before I get in more trouble."

Webb shuffled back home. He didn't know why he'd bothered. Jason would find out that Bree overdosed soon enough, but it wouldn't help her now. He wanted to know what would make Bree want to die.

When he got home, Mrs. Brewer's car was in the driveway. The trunk was open, crammed with black garbage bags. Webb saw her scurry out and shove another bag inside.

"Do you need help?" he asked, starting toward her.

"No, thank you, Webster. That was the last one." Her lungs heaved for a new breath.

Webb hesitated in the driveway. "What are you doing with the bags?"

"Bree is going to stay with my cousin in Ohio. Back in her old school, with her old friends. It's what's best for her," Mrs. Brewer said, not looking Webb in the eyes.

Each bag, haphazardly packed with Bree's stuff, made Webb feel like she was throwing her daughter away.

"Can I at least say goodbye?"

Mrs. Brewer shook her head. "I'm sorry, but I'm picking her up, and we are leaving from Glendale."

And just like that, she was a memory. A trivia question. A whisper that grew so soft, no one could remember what was said, except for Webb. He thought about her every day.

CHAPTER THIRTY-EIGHT - BRENT AND CHRIS' BASEMENT, TYRONE, PENNSYLVANIA

June 22, 2007

Summer break, finally. In the months after she left, the chatter quieted and Webb's finger healed. He could play guitar again and passed his driver's test. On a manic whim, his stepdad bought an old Chevy Prism for Webb's eighteenth birthday. He should have been happy, but it all seemed like a waste without Bree.

Webb heard from her sporadically. At first she sent a letter almost every day, but the mailbox had disappointed him for the last month. She called him twice, but he was with Brent and Chris both times. He picked up a calling card at Sheetz, planning to call her back, but he didn't know what to say.

He finally got up the courage to send her a CD of the songs the band recorded in Brent and Chris' basement. He'd written every song but one. He waited until he was sure she'd received the disc before he called.

"Hey, it's Webb," he said as soon as she answered.

"I know your voice," she said. He could tell that her lips were pulling into her coy smile on the other end of the phone.

"I thought I'd help you out, just in case you forgot about us." He wanted to ask her about the CD right away, but he filled a few minutes with innocuous updates from school.

"Merilee and Cole are dating."

"Ouch. Who are you hanging out with now?" she asked.

"Brent and Chris." He took a breath. "Did you get the package I sent?"

"Oh, yeah. I thought the songs were really good," she said, sounding distracted.

"I wrote most of them," Webb said, hoping it would encourage her to share more. A long pause made Webb wonder if the call had gone dead.

"They'd be great if you found someone with a better voice to sing them. The dude singing is… meh."

Bree's words became a giant magnet extracting his newly metallic heart through his stomach. He shook off his falling hopes.

"Well, it's just a demo. Shitty recording equipment and, you know…"

"No, I get it. Like I said, the songs are good, but you should find another lead singer. Who's singing? That Chris kid?" she asked, blinding Webb with another blow.

"I have to go, but I'm glad you got the CD," he said.

He didn't call her again. Instead, he'd write her a letter back every few weeks. She'd make fun of him for not having a computer. "Why can't you email me?" she'd ask. But the truth was, he liked the letters more. She had touched them, folded them, licked the envelopes.

Secretly, he waited to hear his window squeak up and for Bree to climb into bed next to him. But to his disappointment, he woke up alone every morning. Someday, she'd have to come back. Then again, maybe she'd be like Zoe and never come home.

Since he didn't have to bum a ride with his mom, Webb spent his extra time in Brent and Chris' basement. He got a part-time job at a music store in Altoona to pay for gas, new strings, and a bag of weed every now and then. He'd spent the last few months in a cloudy stupor.

"Dude. You are going to freak out when you hear this," Chris said, putting his feet up on the coffee table. A bag of Cheetos crunched under the heel of his combat boot. "Tell him, Brent."

"You know that guy with the cell phone stores?" Brent asked. Webb shook his head.

"He has those really annoying commercials…" Chris hinted.

"Oh yeah, the Cellular Station guy?" Webb said, nodding. He could already tell this was going to be one of those winding, hour-long stories.

"His brother owns a big farm or something. And…"

"And," Chris piped in, "they're having a music festival there next month."

"And…?" Webb prodded.

"You know that metal band from Altoona who thinks they're Metallica? What's their name?" Chris asked.

"MetalEdge," Brent answered.

"Right. They broke up last week. And now there's an open spot that they need to fill."

"And?" Webb prodded again.

"We're going to take their place."

"Shut up. Are you serious?"

"He really liked our demo. And the guy who lives next door builds motorcycles for Lenny Kravitz or some shit. So he might be able to hook us up with a producer."

Webb couldn't decide if he was more worried about Lenny Kravitz or about playing live for an audience. It was one thing to fool around in the basement, but actually play for people? He didn't think they were ready.

The basement sessions had helped Webb grow comfortable enough to sing in front of Brent and Chris, but when he thought of singing in front of strangers he panicked.

No matter how many times Chris said, "You have the best voice and they're your songs…" Webb only heard Bree. Her criticism erased Chris's claims.

"I'm not a performer."

"Too bad," Chris said. "One of us has to do it."

They had ten good songs by then, but it wasn't enough to fill a set. So they learned covers while Webb tried to write a few more songs.

"I think it's a cop-out," Brent said.

"Maybe *you* should write some decent songs then," Chris said.

Brent scowled. He had written as many songs as Webb, but even he knew they were terrible.

"I don't know. I think it could be cool to play a few covers. Maybe when they hear us from across the field they'll have to come and see if it's really Coldplay," Webb said.

"No one is going to mistake you for Chris Martin," Brent snorted.

DURING THE weeks before the show, they met any time the three of them could get together. One Saturday afternoon, Webb walked into the basement. A guy he didn't recognize was sitting on the couch, his legs splayed out like he felt right at home.

"Webb, meet our bassist, Garrett," Brent said.

Chris shot an apologetic look at Webb, who tried not to let the new guy see how left out he felt.

Garrett stood. Even though Webb was almost six feet tall, Garrett towered over him by at least five inches.

"I didn't know we were looking for a bassist," Webb said. "Where'd you meet?"

He really wanted to ask why he wasn't consulted.

"At Guitar Center in State College. I was trying out a new bass, and we all sat down and jammed," Garrett said.

"He's really good," Chris said. "And he has recording software on his computer."

"Yeah, I'm going to bring it over so we can record another demo," Garrett added.

"What's wrong with our demo?" Webb asked.

"You can hear my mom yelling for us to 'keep it down' in the background," Brent said.

"I thought it added something interesting to the song," Webb argued.

"Well, this is my band, and I want a new demo," Brent said.

"Stop saying it's *your* band," Chris said.

"The demo sucks. I can record everything separately. Isolate each instrument and tweak it. It makes a difference," Garrett explained.

"Fine, whatever," Webb said.

Man, he already hated this guy.

They started practicing. And as much as Webb hated to admit it, Garrett's bass lines added a polish that was missing in their music. There wasn't much to his personality, but the band didn't need more personality.

CHAPTER THIRTY-NINE - A FIELD NEAR BALD EAGLE, PENNSYLVANIA

August 11, 2007

 It wasn't really a stage, more like a box of wood slapped on top of the muddy ground. At least there was power and a small PA system they could use. They couldn't afford their own yet.

Webb counted a total of six stages that dotted the perimeter of the field and a large, respectable stage in the middle. Campers were starting to set up a tent city around the big stage. As they claimed spots, a few organizers quickly roped off an area to create a place for the audience to stand and dance.

As Webb and the guys unloaded their gear, a girl with wild curls stopped to investigate.

"That cord isn't grounded," she said, pointing to an extension cord plugged into a splitter, then into a surge protector.

"So?" Chris asked.

"So, you could die from electrocution or blow up my PA. I only care about the second scenario," she said, unplugging the cord and rearranging power supplies until she was happy.

"Who is this bitch?" Brent said under his breath.

"This bitch's name is Charlotte," she said. "And I'd be happy to take my bitch-infused equipment back and let you all fuck off and find your own sound."

And for the first time in seven years, Webb noticed another girl. Looking at Charlotte hurt.

THEY DIDN'T perform until the next day, but they quietly played without amps that night. As soon as people stopped to listen, Webb's throat closed up. His voice became froggy, like a bubble got stuck over his larynx.

"Dude, what's wrong with you?" Chris asked.

"I told you, I can't sing in front of people. I get too freaked out."

"Everyone thinks that," Brent said.

"Yeah, but this is actually true. Someone else has to sing. I can't do it. I'll fuck it up."

Brent squeezed his eyes shut in frustration. "Unless Webb is going to sing 'Rainbow Connection,' I agree."

"Brent, can you take over?" Garrett asked.

Brent looked like he was thinking about objecting, but then shrugged. "Whatever," he said. "I'll sing. Lead singers always get the hottest chicks anyway."

As soon as Brent took over the vocals, the dynamic shifted. He could sing Webb's songs better than Webb could sing them. He made them come alive with emotion—the things Webb was afraid to feel. It was like Brent knew the extra depth Webb's words needed, where to punctuate, where to linger. When the first song was over, they stood, staring at the ground.

"That was intense," Garrett said.

All Webb and Chris could do was nod and say, "Yeah."

Brent, Chris, and Webb had planned to share an old Boy Scout tent that Chris found in the garage. It would have been a tight fit for two, but three teenage boys barely fit width-wise and their feet poked out of the door. Garrett insisted on setting up his sleeping bag outside on the ground.

In the middle of the night, Webb crawled out with his sleeping bag. Webb didn't need to climb inside the bag. Even at midnight, it was eighty degrees and humid.

He lay under the stars, too nervous to sleep. Every time he thought he was drifting off, he would imagine being in front of strangers with his words and notes projecting across the field. Anxiety would jerk him awake. What if he forgot the chords? What if he played the wrong part of the song? What if no one stopped to listen?

After tossing with worry for an hour, he got up and wandered around the encampment. More tents had claimed spots, people were passing bowls around small campfires, cooking meats or veggie burgers on camp stoves, and in the far end of the camp, a giant bonfire burned.

Webb made his way toward it, just to observe. He didn't want to join in or even talk to anyone, but he didn't want to be alone either. He stood on the fringe of the fire, behind a ring of kids in tie-dye shirts who were sitting on the ground. One of them strummed a guitar and sang "Creep" by Radiohead.

He pulled out his one-hitter and ground the tip into his dwindling stash of weed. He'd taken a big puff when he felt someone slide next to him.

"Got any of that for me?"

He shrugged, still holding in the hit, and passed the dugout and cigarette-shaped pipe to Charlotte.

They didn't look at each other as they passed the pipe back and forth. Alone together, it felt perfectly comfortable to Webb.

"So what's your deal?" Charlotte asked.

"What do you mean?"

"Are you gay?"

"Excuse me?"

"I mean, it's cool if you are. Actually, I'm kind of into girls these days, just trying it out…"

"Why, do I seem like I'm gay?" Webb pulled his eyebrows together. Maybe it was the weed, but he felt suddenly lost in the conversation. Lost in time.

"I keep waiting for you to hit on me," she said and laughed. "I'm usually a good judge of things like that."

"Do you want me to hit on you?"

She pushed her curls back with a frustrated hand. "No, but it's weird that you're not doing it."

"That's pretty fucked-up," Webb said. Then they both erupted with laughter. "But I still think you're cool."

"What's your name again?" He had never told her, but he didn't say that.

"Webster, but everyone calls me Webb."

"Well, Webb. It's been nice. Thanks for the smoke. I'm tired, so I have to say, 'fuck off.'"

"Wait. What?" Had he done or said something wrong?

"I'm tired," she repeated.

"No, why did you tell me to fuck off?"

"Oh," she laughed. "I don't say the G-word. It's bad luck for me," she said over her shoulder as she started back toward the campsites.

"The G-word as in goodbye?"

"That's the one," she said.

"That's weird, but ok. Fuck off, Charlotte," Webb said with a smile and watched her walk away. Something inside him shifted. For the first time in years, the tickling aches and longing felt different.

CHAPTER FORTY - A FIELD NEAR BALD EAGLE, PENNSYLVANIA

August 12, 2007

Webb fell asleep at the base of a tree, listening to stumbling renditions of songs from all over the music spectrum—from The Eagles to The Shins. As he drifted off, he thought about Charlotte—her sharp confidence, the words "fuck off."

The bonfire died into ash, but the smoke from its rage covered Webb. It had soaked into his shirt, pants, and hair. He trudged back to the campsite. Brent lounged on Webb's sleeping bag with one leg casually propped up as he entertained two girls.

"That didn't take long," Webb said to Chris as he approached their camp.

"I think we're all going to regret this," Chris said.

Webb detected something he'd never noticed before; Chris seemed jealous of his brother. Brent was a few inches taller, his skin was clear, his teeth a little whiter and straighter. If Chris was the generic brother, Brent was the brand-name version. And now he held the coveted position of lead singer.

"Come on, Brent. Let's go through the set one more time," Chris said.

After his new harem skittered away, Brent announced that he'd come up with a name for the band. Their demo tape showed the name "BCWG," but overnight that had become unacceptable.

"What about the name TempFive?" Brent asked.

"It's a stupid name," Chris argued.

"It sounds like we're a boy band," Webb said.

"Isn't every band using numbers in their names now? And shouldn't it be TempFour?" Garrett asked.

"No, that sounds too much like tempura. TempFive is better. Unless you're cool with The Brent Matthews Band."

They all scowled.

"What do we say when someone asks how we came up with our name?" Webb asked.

"We say Brent forced it on us, and everyone hates it except him," Chris said.

Webb laughed, but Brent glared at his brother. "It's off the table unless you can come up with a better name."

No one came up with a better name.

CHAPTER FORTY-ONE - I-99, OUTSIDE BEDFORD, PENNSYLVANIA

January 23, 2016

A high-pitched, whistling sound was coming from where the Camaro had hit the guardrail. Webb turned up the radio, but he could still hear it, or thought he could hear it. The noise burrowed its way into his ear.

He slowed, telling himself it was because he was afraid there was something wrong with the car. Despite his reduced speed, he was moving forward. Getting closer. The GPS counted the miles and minutes. With each change, Webb resisted the urge to redirect his course east to Philadelphia.

He was trying to create order in chaos. Trying to make sense, to cope with the inevitable. She was going to die, if she hadn't died already. What would his world be like?

He had invested so much hope that someday she would understand that they had to be together. That eventually they'd both come to an agreement and live happily ever after. Married. Kids. A quiet house in the middle of nowhere or a brownstone in Brooklyn.

Although this dream had evaporated into mist years ago, he had never been able to wash the residue away. It created an invisible shield, a repellant that guarded him from the girls who wanted to be anointed in his bed.

As he pushed farther north, the roads thickened with snow. The flakes were coming down heavy enough for him to switch the windshield wipers on again. The cheap sunglasses he'd picked up at the gas station reduced the glare, but his vision seemed blurred by imperfections in the lenses.

The phone interrupted the song that was playing. Webb glanced at the console to see if he recognized the number. It wasn't Charlotte's, though. He answered, bracing himself for bad news.

"Webster?" It was his mom. "I've been trying to call that number you left on my machine, but you didn't pick up."

He was afraid to speak, afraid to listen. For too many seconds, Webb felt like he was hanging in space with a dwindling oxygen supply.

"I'm almost there. The GPS says fifteen more miles," he said finally.

"She's stable. No need to rush."

She's still alive.

Webb rubbed his throat. "Good, that's good, right?"

"It's very good. They think they have a donor. She's hanging in there."

"They have a donor?"

"There was a big accident last night," she said. "So promise me you'll be careful, please. I don't need two people I love in here."

"I promise. I'll see you soon."

With the decreased urgency, Webb felt like he could see better, concentrate easier, but that left room for him to speculate what would happen when he saw her.

CHAPTER FORTY-TWO - A FIELD NEAR BALD EAGLE, PENNSYLVANIA

August 12, 2007

Webb felt stupid getting up and standing on a piece of wood to play to an empty crowd. It wasn't even noon yet. Most campers, having just passed out a few hours earlier, were still sleeping.

They called this time slot the breakfast shift—a throwaway slot that opened for the opening act's openers. The breakfast shift bands were one step above the campfire circles singing cover songs. At least it was a paying gig.

They took their places without an introduction. Webb could tell the rest of the band was disappointed by the lack of fanfare, but he was relieved. Without an audience it wouldn't be such a big deal when one of them screwed up.

It didn't take long for Chris to make the first flub, dropping his stick after hitting a cymbal too hard. Webb followed shortly after. His sweaty hands slipped on the neck of his guitar as he played. The slight delay threw him off-time, summoning an annoyed look from Brent. When Brent flashed a third reprimand, Webb wanted to shout that it wasn't like anyone was listening.

During the first set, which was all covers, a few people stopped on their way to the port-o-johns. That was one bonus of their location. Everybody had to go to the bathroom. And when they did, they passed TempFive on the way.

"Dude. Get yourself together," Brent said when they took a five-minute break between sets. Brent's voice carried a hard layer of arrogance.

"I can't help it. My hands are sweaty," Webb said. Webb and Chris exchanged looks and walked back onstage to get in their places.

After a few minutes, Webb's heart slowed and the ease of performing set in. Then a crowd started to gather. At first most passersby only stayed for a minute or until the end of the song that captured them. Then they would shuffle away to the bathrooms or back to their campsites. But then, one by one, they started to stay. Soon there were twenty people in front of the speakers, swaying or singing along. And the larger the crowd became, the more people stopped.

Webb watched them reacting to his songs, memorizing the hook by the second verse and singing it back to him, well, actually back to Brent. He walked the tenuous line of appreciation and remorse as he watched Brent singing *his* words, seducing the audience with *his* melodies. Webb watched Brent forget that the songs belonged to Webb.

His fury grew and then suddenly stopped. He saw Charlotte in the back of the crowd with an older guy. For a second, Webb thought he looked like Lenny Kravitz. But since the crowd seemed more interested in soaking in the songs than looking at the dude next to Charlotte, it probably wasn't. Still, that's where Webb kept his focus.

After the show, they scrambled to clear out their gear while the next band started setting up. Once everything was packed in Brent's car, the three of them returned to listen to the next band. As soon as they approached, the crowd dispersed away from the stage and formed a circle around them.

People were coming up to them, saying, "You guys are really good," or asking, "Where else do you play?" Brent turned on his charisma, seeming gracious—almost modest. While Webb and Chris lingered in the background, Brent accepted invitations to different campsites and girls' tents.

To celebrate, they went deep into the tent villages and hung out with their new fans. They drank and talked and wandered around. They checked out the other acts.

When Webb didn't feel like entertaining anymore, he left Brent in a school of girls. Before disappearing, he asked Chris if he wanted to go back to the campsite, but Chris seemed content circling the perimeter, trying to catch the chum.

Webb told himself he wanted to escape the frenzy around Brent as he aimed his steps in the direction of Charlotte's campsite. But really, he wanted to see her again.

The exact location of her camper was unknown. Last night, she had waved her hands in the direction of the hill to the left of the bonfire, but other than that, Webb didn't know where it was or what it looked like. It didn't really matter. He wasn't looking for her as much as he was looking for an excuse to be off-duty now.

He didn't have to search too hard for Charlotte. He heard her laugh before he saw her. It was a deep, throaty laugh that boomed with confidence. Unlike Bree's, it was genuine. The kind of laugh that declared, "I don't care about sounding like anyone but myself."

Charlotte was standing next to the guy from earlier. Up close, he didn't look like Lenny Kravitz anymore.

"This is Webb, he plays guitar for the band that replaced MetalEdge," Charlotte said.

Her uncle extended his hand. "Dawes Green, nice to meet you."

Webb tried to place where he'd heard her uncle's name as they shook hands.

"How old are you? Fifteen?" Dawes asked.

Embarrassment flowed relentlessly under Webb's skin. "Eighteen," he said.

"You have a decent sound, but your songs are surprisingly good for a kid," Dawes said. "Good enough to be on a bigger stage. Who writes them?"

"I do," Webb answered, suddenly shy from the praise.

"That's good. That's really good." He studied Webb for a moment then excused himself. "I've gotta run and make an appearance. It was nice to meet you, Webb."

"He was really impressed with you guys," Charlotte said once he was gone.

"Why does his name sound familiar?"

"My uncle *is* Launch Records," Charlotte explained and rattled off a list of bands successful enough to be scrawled on shoes and backpacks of kids who discovered pre-sellout genius.

"Holy shit."

"Right?" She pulled out a bowl, took a long drag, and then blew a cloud of smoke straight into the darkening sky. Music from the main stage echoed all around, clashing into a discordant symphony with the songs blasting from campfires that were popping up. The result was sometimes transcendent and other times screeched like a shopping cart with a rattling wheel.

"So what does that mean?" Webb asked, taking a hit and mimicking the way Charlotte blew it to the Milky Way.

"He doesn't do your genre, but he knows people who do. The music industry is surprisingly small. He could help you get a real demo out and maybe even give it to the right people."

Webb should have been excited, but he felt heavy inside. Playing the fifth stage at a Central Pennsylvania music festival was a lot different than getting a record deal and touring in real clubs... the panic nudged his heartbeat. Webb had to stop thinking about it.

"I don't think we're ready to do that," he said.

"It doesn't happen overnight. I mean, it could take years until everything falls into place. But the music industry is for the young. You have to have a plan and make the most of right now."

"Do you have a plan?" he asked, already knowing the answer.

"Of course I do. By the time I'm nineteen, I'll be on tour, managing a band. By the time I'm thirty, I'll start my own label."

Suddenly he felt inadequate. By the time she was nineteen? He thought she was in her twenties.

"How old are you?" Webb asked.

"I just turned eighteen, so time is running out."

Webb squinted, trying to figure out if he had heard her correctly. Was she saying that a clock was ticking somewhere with an expiration date for his chance to escape Glen Hope? Wasn't this a conversation that happened later in life?

"I think I still have a few years to worry about missing my dreams," he said, but when he heard his words, he thought of his mother. How under the layers of defeat there was once a girl who thought she could be an actress or a model. He could remember her going to photo shoots for local department store ads when he was little, but he couldn't remember when she gave up her dream. It had slowly procrastinated itself away, like the old house on the corner of his street that the county condemned and tore down last year.

Maybe he wouldn't notice his dreams had changed until it was too late. Maybe one day, his part-time job at Guitar Center would become full-time. The urgent desire to leave Glen Hope would turn into acceptance. He would live each day not realizing he was trapped in an inescapable Glen Hope life.

"Where'd you go?" Charlotte asked, waving a hand in front of his face.

"Nowhere." Webb chuckled and added, "I'm just tired. You're right, though."

"I usually am," she said.

The corner of her mouth inched up like a window shade that exposed one jagged incisor. Webb noticed it stuck out a little farther than the rest of her teeth. He smiled back.

"So what's your deal, anyway? Do you have a girlfriend?"

"Nah. I mean, I did, but we broke up a few months ago." He took a swig of a beer that some kid in a Phish shirt had offered him earlier. It was warm, but he felt like he had to do something with his mouth. Her question seemed too personal.

"Did she cheat on you?" she pried.

"No," Webb said softly, almost as a huff.

"Did you cheat on her?"

"Why does someone have to be cheating on someone else?"

"They don't, but you're not acting like it ended civilly. So it has to be cheating, or something bad."

"I was in love with someone else…" he said and then wished he hadn't.

Charlotte arched an eyebrow. "Really? Do tell." She took a big drag.

"The girl who lived across the street from me. We had a really weird and complicated thing. It doesn't matter, because she moved back to Ohio."

"So you lost your girlfriend and the girl you broke up with her for?"

"I didn't exactly break up with her. She broke up with me, but not because of that. It's a messed-up situation, and honestly, I don't want to talk about it."

"No pressure. I get it." She looked at her feet, maybe because she was thinking, or maybe because she felt bad for digging into his past. Webb wasn't sure about anything Charlotte did. She didn't fit the shape for any girl he had ever met.

"I just broke up with someone a few weeks ago. She was so fucking cool and bizarre, super-talented but a total mess. I can't deal with that level of maintenance. I found her in her closet, passed out on pills. Just un-fucking cool," Charlotte said.

"That's so weird."

"Not really. So many people are getting sucked into pills."

"No, I mean that's kind of what happened to Bree, the girl…"

Charlotte's eyes invited him to confide. It took him a few moments of silent struggle to give in. Webb told her about finding Bree, and the overdose, and her mom, and the garbage bags. Charlotte listened. Not judging or even trying to understand, but empathizing.

They lay back on the grass, looking at the stars. Webb felt the ground beneath him dampen with morning. And for the first time in months, he didn't wish Bree were there next to him. For the first time in months, Webb felt content.

CHAPTER FORTY-THREE - GLEN HOPE, PENNSYLVANIA

August 17, 2007

Webb woke to red-and-white lights reflecting their rotation across his walls. At first he thought it was the police outside, maybe the fire company. But he didn't hear sirens. He padded over to his window, looking across the road to Bree's house. All the lights were on and the front door was open. An ambulance idled in the street.

It was still early enough to be dark, so Webb had to squint to see the shadowy figures walking down the driveway, rolling a stretcher out to the street. When the streetlight hit it, Webb saw a lumpy white sheet. It was a body. The two paramedics weren't in a rush to roll the gurney into the back of their ambulance.

Webb ran into the hall to wake his mother. "I think someone died," he said after knocking in her doorway.

She sat up in bed. "Why do you think that?"

"There's an ambulance outside the Brewers' house, and it looks like they just pulled a body out," Webb explained.

His mom cinched her robe, and they both walked downstairs to the front window. Mrs. Brewer stood in the street and watched as they loaded Mr. Brewer's body inside.

As he watched the ambulance pull away, Webb wondered how

Mr. Brewer died and how Bree would feel about it. Her dad was the reason she left, the reason she tried to kill herself, wasn't he?

WEBB FLOATED through work, partially in a haze from lack of sleep, partially because he wanted to know when she would be back. Yes, *when* she would come back, because she could finally come home.

Webb didn't want to wait for the news to trickle down to him. He wanted to go home sick from work, knock on the Brewers' door and find out exactly when Bree would return, but he kept stringing guitars and helping people pick out amps.

When he got home, his mom was gone, but her car was in the driveway. A few minutes after his Hot Pocket came out of the microwave, she came through the door.

"Where were you?" he asked, more curious than demanding.

"I went over to console Mrs. Brewer."

Webb's mouth was full of hot cheese and ham. He blew the steam out while asking, "Wha ha-enned?"

"Heart attack." His mom looked away and rubbed her face, as if she was trying to wipe off the emotional residue that had built up on her skin from being over there.

"Does Bree know?" he asked.

"Yes, she knows. She's coming back this weekend for the funeral."

Webb swallowed the bite of Hot Pocket. It burned his throat going down. "Just for the funeral, or is she moving back?"

"She's moving back," his mom said and then walked out into the living room. She was acting weird, but Webb was too distracted by the news to care too much about it. His entire body smiled inside. She would be across the street again. He had a car. Jason was dating Hailey. He was in a band. Everything could be perfect now.

Plus, her dad was gone. That had to make her happier, right? Maybe somehow she'd be normal now. Or just normal enough to be ok, but still quirky enough to be interesting. The details didn't matter. Bree would be back in his universe soon.

CHAPTER FORTY-FOUR · GLEN HOPE, PENNSYLVANIA

August 19, 2007

He didn't want it to look like he was waiting for her, but he was. Bree took a Greyhound bus from Columbus to Altoona. Her mom had picked her up at least an hour ago. It almost felt like he was waiting to see who would climb into the back seat with him the day they met.

He planned to casually walk out as their car pulled up and pretend to be on his way somewhere. He'd offer to help with her bags, and he wouldn't let her get away again. He'd tell her how he felt.

He checked his hair in the mirror and then did a close-up scan of his face. There were a few blotches on his chin line. As he shaved the errant hairs, the phone rang.

"Webster," his mom called up.

He picked up the extension in the hall.

"Hey," Charlotte said. "What are you doing right now?"

"Uh," he stalled, unsure how much he should tell her.

It felt weird to say something about waiting for Bree. There was no good reason for him to hide the details from Charlotte. Nothing was going on between them, or between him and Bree, but it still felt wrong. That didn't make any sense, Webb thought.

"Nothing, just hanging out. Why?"

"My uncle gave his friend your demo. He's in State College today and wants to meet you. Well, you and the rest of the band."

Why was she coming to Webb with this news and not Brent or Chris?

The same reason that Webb didn't want to tell her that Bree was back.

"It's a good idea," she coaxed.

"Sure. I'll tell the guys."

"I'm near Houtzdale. I can swing by and get you," she said.

He gave her the best directions he could. "After the Sunoco, veer off to the left."

"Got it. Tell them to meet us at The Cell Block on College Avenue. See you in ten minutes. Fuck off, Webb."

"Fuck off, Charlotte," he replied and hung up.

"Webster! That's a terrible thing to say to someone," his mom said, smacking the back of his head. He hadn't heard her come up the stairs.

"No, that's what we do…"

"Find something else to do then."

He shrugged her off and called Brent to relay the information. Webb heard a car rolling to a stop outside. He ran out to meet Charlotte, but it wasn't her. Mrs. Brewer and Bree had pulled into their driveway and were getting out of the car. Webb waved as he walked across the lawn and into the street.

It looked like she had smudged charcoal under her eyes. Her cheeks were sharp, not like the healthy, round mounds he remembered. But despite her gaunt appearance, she was smiling.

Mrs. Brewer struggled with Bree's suitcase. It flopped on the ground as she dragged it from the car up the walk.

"Here, let me help you with that," Webb offered and pulled the suitcase upright. He carried it inside as Bree grabbed her purse and a half-eaten bag of peanut M&Ms from the front seat.

As he held the front door open for Mrs. Brewer, Charlotte pulled up. Webb hesitated on the porch before he lifted the suitcase over the threshold. He tucked it next to the coat rack and rushed back outside.

"I gotta go, but we'll catch up later?"

Bree nodded. She didn't hide her disappointment as Webb passed her to duck into Charlotte's Corolla.

"Is that her?" Charlotte asked as soon as he closed the door.

"Yeah," Webb said, waving out of the passenger-side window.

Bree responded with a fragile wave that went limp before the car was out of view.

"I thought she was in Ohio."

"Her dad died. She came back for the funeral."

"Fuck. That's awful."

"Yeah, I guess."

Webb sank back into the seat and distracted himself with a conversation about how many states Charlotte had visited. Thirty-three.

"I can't believe that you've never been out of Pennsylvania," Charlotte said. "How is that even possible?"

Webb shrugged. "I don't know. We don't go anywhere."

"Haven't you ever been on vacation?"

"I went camping at Raystown Lake with my friend Jason and his family." Webb started to feel embarrassment snake its way from his forehead to his cheeks.

Charlotte opened her eyes as wide as they could go. "I don't mean to sound like an asshole; it's just surprising."

"I know. It's ok, really," Webb said.

"In a few months you'll be so sick of crossing state lines, it won't even be a big deal," she said.

"I don't think that could ever happen."

"Going on tour or getting sick of being on the road?"

"Both."

"Do you have any idea of how good you are?" she asked.

"I work with incredible musicians—at Guitar Center. It doesn't matter how good you are. No one has ever walked in while they're demoing a Strat and said, 'Here's a record deal.'"

"You don't give yourself enough credit. Your songs are scary good."

Webb rolled his eyes, but inside he basked in her praise.

Charlotte parked in front of McClanahan's on College Avenue. Brent, Chris, and Garrett were waiting on the front steps of the bar, looking eager and curious. Webb hadn't known what to tell them on the phone, so he made it sound cryptic enough to make them come right away.

He said, "We have a once-in-a-lifetime chance. Meet me at the Cell Block in State College in thirty minutes." Ok, maybe it was more than cryptic.

Chris stood and walked toward them. "What's going on?"

"My uncle hooked you up. You're meeting with Parse Daily," Charlotte said.

"Parse Daily? You're full of shit," Garrett said.

"Who the fuck is Parse Daily, and why should I care?" Brent said. Webb was wondering the same thing.

"He's Dr. Dre for music like ours," Garrett said. "Which is why I highly doubt he'd be at the Cell Block waiting to meet us."

"Well, he is," Charlotte said. "He's also a dickhead, but my uncle said he's starting his own label and looking for bands like TempFive. So act fucking cool."

She led them to a stairwell next to the club and knocked on a door that blended in with the wall. A few seconds later, a bouncer pushed it open, almost knocking Brent to the ground. The bouncer didn't say anything; he just jerked his head to the left as a signal to come inside.

They followed behind him. Webb tried not to let his amazement show as they trekked through the club. He felt too young to be there. Charlotte looked the bouncer in the eye and asked him for a bottle of water.

The bouncer slid behind the bar and filled a cup with ice. Charlotte stopped him and asked, "Don't you have any bottles?"

He sighed and dumped the ice back in the bin. When he left to find a bottle, Charlotte turned to them.

"Act extremely uninterested in everything. Let me do the talking." She paused, looking around. "And no matter what, just go along with whatever I'm doing. He likes your music, but he wants to judge your vibe."

Webb fought a scowl. He didn't want to be judged, even if it did mean a record deal.

The bouncer returned with a bottle of water for Charlotte and mumbled something about Parse being out in a minute. They sat at the bar. Chris and Brent played with their new phones, flipping them open and closed, taking grainy pictures of each other.

A short, nerdy, bald dude with intentionally ugly glasses and skinny jeans approached them with quick steps. Charlotte headed him off and introduced herself first, then the band.

"I really liked your sound. How do you write?" Parse asked. "Is it a group effort?"

"No, Webb writes the songs," Charlotte answered, pointing to him.

"I like them," he said to Charlotte, pulling out a card. "Call this number and schedule some time to cut a demo. And tell your uncle I'll give him a call."

THEY HELD the explosion of celebration until they were a few blocks away from the bar. Brent kept repeating, "Holy shit. Did that just happen?"

Webb locked his arms around Charlotte's neck.

"You're fucking magic, Char," he said and smacked his lips on her cheek.

She pushed him away and said, "I know."

CHARLOTTE'S CAR rolled to a stop in front of Webb's house. They had exhausted their excitement on the drive back by recounting the experience play-by-play. For the last fifteen minutes of the ride, they basked in the afterglow of their success. They were going to Philly to record a real demo.

"So was this part of your plan?" Webb asked Charlotte.

"Yep. I think you guys are going to be big, and I want to be a part of it."

"Do you know anything about bands making it big?" Webb teased.

"You know Coldplay?"

He tilted his head down and took a sarcastic breath. "That's a stupid question."

"My uncle got their demo when we were in London. We were on our way to dinner, and he popped into a pub to hear them play live for a few minutes. My mom and I had to wait at the door, because I was like, seven years old, but I spent the whole time wishing I could go inside because their music made my scalp shiver."

"Your scalp shivered?" Webb barked out a laugh. "What does that prove?"

"The same thing happened when I heard your music. Like I said, you're going to be big, and I want to be a part of that."

"What are you going to do?"

"I told you, I'm going to be your manager."

"Considering the fact that you're the only reason we're talking about this, I'm sure no one will have a problem with that."

"I know. Now fuck off, Webb. I have to get home."

Webb chuckled as he got out of the car and started toward his front door.

"Hey!" He stopped at the sound of Bree's voice. She was jogging toward him, her feet in furry sock slippers that were soaking up the water from puddles on the road.

"Hey," Webb said, feeling like he'd been caught doing something wrong.

"Where did you have to go?"

"Oh, my friend Charlotte got us a meeting with this producer from Philly. He wants to help us make a demo."

"Seriously? That's great." She didn't sound like she meant it.

"Yeah, well I guess we'll see." Webb changed the subject. "How are you doing? I mean with your dad and everything?"

Her face turned chipper. "I'm ok. My mom's a mess, but more because she's alone than because she misses him. And she has the thermostat set at, like, fifty degrees, just because she can. He hated air conditioning." She looked back at her house and then leaned forward. "I think she's kind of relieved not to have to take care of him anymore. Is that bad to say?"

Webb smiled. "No. Well, maybe around some people."

Bree shifted her feet, hopping from one foot to the other like she was nervous, or maybe because her soggy socks were bothering her.

"Do you want to come in and hang out?" he asked.

"I have to, you know, hang out with my mom."

"Maybe tomorrow or something?"

"Can't. The funeral is tomorrow. But you should come—I mean, if you want to. It's at three at Gibbon's in Coalport."

"Of course I'll come," Webb said.

A coy, grateful smile inched across her face. She stepped forward and kissed his cheek. As soon as her lips touched his skin, Webb remembered exactly why he had obsessed about her for so many years. He felt the roots of his hair vibrate. He understood what Charlotte meant when she heard Coldplay. Life with Bree was big, and Webb wanted to be a part of it.

CHAPTER FORTY-FIVE - GIBBON'S FUNERAL HOME, COALPORT, PENNSYLVANIA

August 20, 2007

Webb and his mom pulled into the parking lot, which was almost empty except for two other cars—Mrs. Brewer's and a hearse. Webb glanced at the clock. It was almost three.

"Do you think we're the only ones coming?" Webb asked.

"It's possible," his mom said. "Sad, isn't it?"

"Why even bother renting out a funeral home if no one is going to show up?"

"People have to have the opportunity to say goodbye," she said, turning off the ignition.

The rain had stopped, but the ground was still saturated. Webb trudged through the shortcut from the parking lot to the front door. His mom took the long way around to the sidewalk near the street. She frowned at Webb's shoes, which were coated with the kind of mud that looked like butterscotch pudding. He scraped his feet off on the step and then held the door open.

"You've always created your own path, haven't you?" she mused.

They followed the sign that said: *Kenneth F. Brewer Service - Chapel A*. When they walked inside, only Bree, her mom, and a middle-aged woman who looked like a thinner version of Mrs. Brewer were in the room. Webb was relieved to see the casket was closed.

He followed his mom's lead and approached Mrs. Brewer. They exchanged polite greetings and then took two of the twenty seats that were arranged like a horseshoe around a podium.

Bree's back was to him, but he could tell she wasn't paying attention to her mom or the chaplain who just walked in. She was looking straight at the casket. Webb watched her for at least two minutes, and her head didn't move.

He knew that if he could see her face, she'd be glaring through the wood, trying to get her last stabs of hatred in before he was protected by layers of dirt or burned out of existence.

There was no burial. The service seemed too short to be legitimate, but Webb wasn't going to complain. Including this, he had only been to two funerals, the first being his grandfather's, which seemed to last all day.

Once the chaplain closed the ceremony, Mrs. Brewer let out a single cry but quickly sniffled it into silence. Bree gripped her mother's hand. After that, it seemed like their grieving was over. They stood up, walked to the back of the chapel, and stood next to the door.

Webb and his mom approached. When he saw Bree's eyes, his heart churned with sadness. There was something pitiful and searching about her stare.

He attempted to repeat the only words he knew to say at that moment: "I'm sorry for your loss." But it sounded more like, "I'm sorry that you're lost."

MRS. BREWER invited Webb and his mom back to the house. In all the years they had lived across the street, and in all the years he had orbited Bree, he had never been farther than the entryway of the Brewer's house.

He stepped onto the mint-green carpet. It was fluffy, not stomped down like the carpet in Webb's house. In fact, everything in the Brewers' house seemed clean and polished. Things like books and figurines rested in places that appeared to be carved out for them, not haphazardly thrown on a shelf or stacked in a corner.

The adults retreated back into the kitchen, but Webb lingered in the front hall, examining old family pictures hanging on the wall. Her dad was in most of them, smiling, posing. It was obvious they were all before the accident. She came up behind him.

"Thanks for coming over," she said, leaning her head on Webb's shoulder. He wanted to rest his head on hers, to get closer to her, but he stood tall and let her cuddle into him.

"Do you know that I've never been in your house? I mean, since you've lived here, I've never been inside."

"Huh. I never thought about it."

"Seems weird, doesn't it?"

She let out a heavy breath. "I couldn't have company over." She sauntered over to one of the white couches in the living room. "But you're here now. And you can come over anytime you feel like coming over."

"Until you start dating Jason tomorrow."

Webb realized how harsh his words sounded, but he felt like he was stating the obvious. He let his words hang between them without even trying to take them back.

"You think you know me so well," she said, squinting with disgust. "Why do you care anyway? You're the one driving around with some crazy-haired, trendy, crazy person—"

"Charlotte's a really cool girl," he interrupted. "You'd like her."

Her nose twitched. She was seconds away from either storming off or shutting down. "I hate her even more now." She crossed her arms in front of her chest and glared at him.

"You aren't seriously jealous, are you?"

"I don't know. When I thought about coming home, you were the thing that made me smile. But now you're in a band and running around with a girl who looks like she belongs in a maxi pad commercial. And I thought it would be different."

Webb relished her words. For once, it seemed like she cared. "We can still hang out," he offered.

"It's not like I thought it would be. You're just like everyone else."

His elation soured as he remembered all the times he had dreamed up scenarios that would fuse them together. Something that would wash over her, removing the barrier that stopped her from understanding how differently he loved her.

"What do you want me to do, Bree? I thought you didn't want to get stuck here."

She stood strong for a moment, defiant, but then her lower lip quivered until it started to shake tears out of her eyes.

"I hated him more than anything, but it's so stupid. I want you to make it not hurt that he's gone."

Webb pulled her into his chest, resting a hand on her back. He let her cry big, wet stains onto his shirt.

There was nothing he could say, so he simply held her as his confusion and hope boiled inside.

CHAPTER FORTY-SIX · I-99, OUTSIDE ALTOONA, PENNSYLVANIA

January 23, 2016

The GPS directed him to exit in one mile. He had to start paying attention, switching lanes, merging. When he was safely off the highway, Webb pulled into the first parking lot he saw. The GPS corrected his route, trying to coerce him to continue driving toward the hospital. He turned down the volume.

He was less than three miles away from her. He starting pressing icons on the console, looking for a way to make a phone call, shuffling through menus until he found a call history log and pressed Charlotte's number. Error. He grabbed the disposable phone and typed in the number.

She picked up after five rings.

"I can't do this," he said. "I can't see her."

She let out an empathetic sigh. "I know you think that now, but you have to. If you don't, you'll regret it forever."

He sat on the other end of the line in silence.

"Are you at the hospital?"

"Not yet. I'm so close, but I feel like I can't go."

"Where are you?"

"I'm in the parking lot of a Best Buy." He grabbed a chunk of his hair and tugged it, like he could pull his own stupidity out. "This seemed like a better idea when I was a few hundred miles away."

"I know," she said.

She stayed on the line, even though Webb wasn't talking.

CHAPTER FORTY-SEVEN - GOOD PROSPECT STUDIO, PHILADELPHIA, PENNSYLVANIA

September 6, 2007

When Webb pictured what the studio would look like, it didn't look like this. They could have been in an office building, or a college. It felt generic, sterile, uncreative.

He perched on a tall stool with his guitar, waiting for instruction while Chris and Brent helped themselves to a glass from one of the liquor bottles at the back of the room. Nothing about the experience lived up to Webb's expectations. He struggled to look bored and unimpressed when Parse walked through the door.

Parse didn't waste any time getting the band into their places. "We only have two hours, and we've already lost ten minutes," he said. "Get your shit together."

Chris arranged the studio drums to his liking. Brent, Garrett, and Webb took their positions with their instruments.

"These drums are sick," Chris said, hitting a cymbal. "Holy shit. Did you hear that?"

Webb and Brent nodded, warming their fingers up with some scales. An air of fear settled over them. This was real. They weren't practicing on second-hand instruments in a basement. They weren't standing on a piece of plywood playing for a bunch of wannabe hippie kids from Penn State. This was a studio with a real engineer and a kickass drum set. Suddenly

Webb felt enormously underqualified.

"Let's get on with it," Parse said over the intercom.

The four of them looked at each other and positioned themselves to play. They had scribbled out a set list on the way after arguing over which songs to record. If everything went well, they only had time to record three songs. The argument was so heated, Brent's voice was torn and jagged, like he'd inhaled sand.

Parse rubbed his bald head and flipped the intercom switch again. "Let's start with 'Empty Streets.'"

Webb cringed. He hated that song—they all did. Luckily, Brent spoke up before he had to interject.

"We thought we'd go with 'Random Disasters,'" he said.

"No. That's not a good idea. I have the board ready for 'Empty Streets.' Let's go."

Webb and Brent looked at each other, then Webb took his turn to protest.

"We weren't planning on recording that one," he said.

"I don't care if you planned to record it or not. You're fucking recording it. This is your breakout song. So fucking get ready to fucking play the fucking song."

"Who cares. Let's just play the song," Garrett said.

"Listen to your bassist, assholes, and play the song. In five, four..." Parse held up his fingers for three, two, and one. Then they started to play "Empty Streets."

CHARLOTTE WAS waiting outside the studio exactly two hours after they went in. She could have sat in the booth with Parse but didn't want to make them more nervous than they already were. Webb thought her absence had the opposite effect.

"How was it?" she asked, sounding like she was holding her breath as the words came out.

"Amazing," Webb said.

"Really?"

Chris and Brent smiled in agreement. Garrett shrugged in affirmation.

"Unbelievable. At first we didn't want to play 'Empty Streets,' but Parse insisted," Chris said. "Then something happened in there. It was transcendent. And we just got in this flow, and it was perfect. Like every note was perfect. It all came together. I don't know how to explain it."

Charlotte threw her arms around Webb and kissed his cheek. He stepped back, unsure how to react. His cheek heated under the heavy, sticky mark of her lip gloss, but she didn't seem to notice. She kept talking.

"When can we hear it?"

"He said about two weeks," Brent said, looking from Charlotte to Webb and back.

"Perfect! Well, since your work is done, and we have hotel rooms, I thought we could do something fun," Charlotte said. "I have a surprise for you."

CHAPTER FORTY-EIGHT - BEST BUY PARKING LOT, ALTOONA, PENNSYLVANIA

January 23, 2016

"I have a surprise for you," Charlotte said.

Webb slumped his head against the steering wheel and mumbled, "What?"

But before she could answer, three knocks tapped on his window. Webb shot straight up in his seat. His heart strained to push enough blood to his limbs. He was ready to fight or flee until he realized it was her.

"I'm here," she said. A half second later, it echoed through the phone. He didn't feel thankful or grateful, or even relieved to see her. Webb felt saved.

"How did you get here?"

"I rented a car and drove up after the show."

He sprang from the car. He'd never hugged anyone so tightly. And instead of pushing him away like she usually did, Charlotte hugged him back with a force so strong, it was hard for Webb to inhale. He felt her shaking under his arms. It was cold, but she wasn't shivering. Charlotte was crying.

"I thought I was the one who was supposed to be crying," Webb said.

"I know how much she means to you. I mean, fuck, the whole world knows. I want to be here for you, but…"

Webb dug his face into the shoulder of her coat. He didn't know what she was going to say, and he didn't want to hear it.

"Please stop talking," he said.

He stood there, letting her take his fear and hesitation and absorbing Charlotte's courage. She pulled away and wiped her eyes.

"What the fuck did you do to this car?"

"Apparently, rear-wheel drive sucks in the snow."

She transformed back to Charlotte the band manager who kept their shit together.

"I'll drive you to the hospital and take care of this mess later," she said, pointing to the car. "I can't believe you made it here alive."

"Yeah, I fucked it up pretty bad," he said.

"I don't even want to know. I'll figure out a different way to get you to Philly."

"You're not staying?"

She looked away. "I can't."

"What's wrong?" Webb asked.

"You have enough going on. I'll tell you about it later."

CHAPTER FORTY-NINE - SOUTH STREET, PHILADELPHIA, PENNSYLVANIA

September 6, 2007

They wandered into bars and were carded before they could even look inside. After a dozen failed attempts, they found an old Italian restaurant on a side street with a dim, attached lounge. Webb took a seat next to Charlotte. Chris took the other side, but Brent refused to sit down.

"This place blows. Let's find somewhere better," he said, yanking his head toward the door.

"Go ahead, we're staying here," Chris said, not even looking at his brother.

"This isn't my idea of a surprise," Brent said.

"Do what you have to do. But you'll want to meet us at the hotel at six," Charlotte said.

Brent wobbled in the doorway, looking like he couldn't make up his mind to stay or go. But after they all turned back to the bartender and ordered drinks, he walked out.

"Hopefully he'll find somewhere big enough for his ego," Chris said, taking a swig of the Heineken he'd ordered.

"Fuck him," Charlotte said. "We're just getting started."

"To getting started," Chris said, holding up his drink. Webb, Garrett, and Charlotte met his bottle with theirs.

"Let's get some shots," Charlotte said, turning to the bartender before they could agree or argue. "Four shots of Cuervo."

Webb choked down the first one. It burned like hope—a much better idea before it worked its way into reality.

"Is this really the surprise?" Chris asked. "I mean, it's cool to be at a bar with the geriatrics and all, but…"

"No," she answered with a smile and pulled out five lanyards from her purse. "Red Hot Chili Peppers, all-access passes."

"Wait. What?" Webb balked. He reached for a pass to see if it was real.

"Yep. So get ready to see your future," she said and ordered another round of shots.

Chris and Garrett examined the passes like they were artifacts from an ancient temple, but Webb could only think about how much Bree loved the Chili Peppers.

When they walked out of the bar, it was still light out. Webb felt out of context, like walking out of a movie at noon. It felt like it was time for bed, but the night hadn't even started yet. They staggered to the hotel, making a few wrong turns and laughing so hard they had to prop themselves up against the side of a building before stumbling into the hotel lobby.

Brent, who hadn't had as good a time on his own, stewed in a chair. He looked even more put off by their drunken glee.

"What do we have to do?" he asked, trying to rein in their laughter.

"Come on, you big asshole. We'll let you come, even though you're a giant buzzkill," Charlotte said and motioned for them to follow her out to the curb and climb into a minivan cab.

"Wachovia Center, please," she told the cabbie. Webb couldn't help but to be impressed. He'd never called a cab or been in one. To him, this was something that other people did. People who lived in New York, people who were late to a business meeting or trying to catch a plane. But they all rode in the cab, on their way to see a legendary band, with all-access passes, like this was their life now. And for a second, Webb could see the possibility that his life could and would change.

CHAPTER FIFTY - BEST BUY PARKING LOT, ALTOONA, PENNSYLVANIA

January 23, 2016

Charlotte pressed the gas hard, weaving through cars. Every light turned green as they approached, like she had a remote control.

It had to mean something. It had to be a sign that he was supposed to be there. And with each new green light, Webb's hope that Bree would survive grew, but he wasn't as happy as he thought he'd be.

Charlotte came to a stop in front of the main entrance. Webb lingered in the car.

"Good luck in there," she said. "I'll text you and let you know how you're getting to Philly. Don't forget your phone."

He grabbed his phone and suddenly felt reconnected to the world. "You're amazing. You know that, right?"

"Fuck off, Webb."

He braced himself against the cold and called his mom.

"I'm here, but I don't know where to go. How's she doing?"

"She's getting ready to go into surgery."

"That's unbelievable. I'll be right up," he said.

"She's already in pre-op. They're starting the surgery any minute, if they haven't started already. But this is good news."

His face reddened. If he hadn't pulled off the road last night to sleep, or left his phone, or sat in the fucking Best Buy parking lot, maybe he could have seen her. Maybe he could have said what he needed to say. But now she was going into surgery—that she might or might not survive—and he had to wait even longer.

"I'll be right down. I need a cigarette," she said and then hung up.

When she walked out, Webb almost didn't recognize her. Her shoulders curved in, making her back form a harsh "C", and she seemed a few inches shorter.

"You look too skinny, like a heroin addict," she chastised. He could have said the same about her, but he didn't.

"It's hard to eat sometimes." He changed the subject. "How long is the surgery?"

"I don't know, six hours? Eight at the most. I'm glad you're here. Being alone in the waiting room was driving me crazy. Seth went home to change his clothes and take a shower, but I doubt he'll be sober enough to come back."

Webb clenched his teeth together. He'd forgotten about Bree's husband.

"Can I have one of those?" he asked, pointing at her cigarette.

"I thought you quit," she said.

"I stopped buying them. There's a difference."

Webb's mom tapped a Marlboro Gold out of the soft pack and handed it to her son with a lighter. He lit it and looked down at the lighter.

"Are you kidding me?" he asked. "They have TempFive lighters?"

"I got it at Sheetz. I bought all they had." She took another drag. "And the cashier didn't believe that you were my son. She said her cousin went to high school with you and knew someone who knew your first girlfriend, Meredith." She hacked out a laugh. "I assume she meant Merilee."

"Obviously she knows me. I should give you a laminated ID card or something to prove you're my mom," Webb said, taking a drag. The smoke didn't feel as good as it used to, but he kept smoking it.

The small talk tore jagged rips inside Webb. He didn't want to talk about anything serious either, but he'd come all this way.

"So how is she?"

"No news is good news," she said with a shrug.

"Does she know?" he asked.

"That you're paying for everything? Yes. That you're here? No."

"You told her I was paying for this? Mom!"

"She was worrying about it too much, so I told her. I thought it would give her some hope. Help her keep a positive attitude." She smiled, revealing her yellowed teeth. "You shouldn't let this much time go by without seeing your mother."

"I didn't think I was welcome here," he said.

It had been years since Webb left for New York and Gary told him to leave for good, since he said the terrible things to his mom.

Webb stomped out his cigarette on the ground and then picked it up and walked it to the trash can. His mom lit another one.

"It's a long walk up to the waiting room," she said, handing him another cigarette.

CHAPTER FIFTY-ONE - WACHOVIA CENTER, PHILADELPHIA, PENNSYLVANIA

September 6, 2007

They entered through a special VIP gate, bypassing the lines and chaos flooding into the stadium.

"One day, we'll be playing here," Brent said.

"That would scare the shit out of me," Chris said, looking around at all the flood of people in Red Hot Chili Peppers shirts.

"Yeah. People screaming your name, singing your songs… It's a little creepy, don't you think?" Webb said, agreeing with Chris.

"It's baby steps to somewhere like this," Charlotte said. "By the time you make it here, you'll be ready."

"I'd go out there right now," Brent said as they slipped behind a curtain that hid a door to an industrial hallway. They traversed the maze of concrete floors and nicked-up white cinder block walls.

Charlotte took a loud breath. "Ready to meet the band?"

"You don't need to be dramatic," Brent said, pushing past her. "They're dudes like us."

Webb gritted his teeth, wishing they'd left Brent back at the hotel.

The band wasn't in the green room, but a bunch of other fans were. Some had won contests or had parents who were important in Philadelphia. At the far end of the room, Webb saw Parse talking to a guy in dark jeans and a black V-neck shirt. His hair was perfectly messy, his glasses nerdy and ironic.

Parse waved Charlotte over. Brent took the lead, swiping a beer out of an ice bucket along the way.

"Hey, Parse," he said, reaching out his beer-free hand to shake.

"These are the guys I was telling you about," Parse said, ignoring Brent's outstretched hand. "This is my brother, Rex. He's the other half of the label."

Webb and Chris fought off smiles. Of course his brother had an equally ridiculous name.

"Hey. Yeah, your song is catchy," Rex said.

"We're working on a deal for you," Parse said. "So grab a beer and enjoy your front row seats while you think about it."

"You'll be on this stage in a few years," Rex said.

"Cool. Yeah, we'll think about it," Brent said.

Webb swam in the words floating around him. Record deal? Was it really that easy? Weren't they supposed to work harder for something like this?

When they were back by the spread of food and drinks, he leaned in to Chris and Brent. "What's the catch?" he whispered.

"What do you mean? There's no catch. We're fucking lucky and awesome," Brent said, offended that he would question the serendipitous events leading them to stardom.

"It seems too good to be true. And if we're so awesome, maybe we should look around a little more," Webb said.

"Listen, Parse knows what he's doing. It could take years to get another opportunity like this. You have the right sound at the right time, and you know the right people," Charlotte said. She ducked out of their circle and made her way to the bar.

"I think we should do what Parse said. Enjoy the show and make a decision tomorrow," Brent said.

But it wasn't good enough for Webb. The way Brent was talking and acting, the deal was already done. They would have to do what he said.

Somehow, in the months since their first show, TempFive had become Brent's band, and everyone else was just along for the ride.

"I'll see you back at the hotel," Webb said, grabbing a bottle of vodka from the open bar before he walked away.

Charlotte followed him for a few steps. "Where are you going?"

He stopped abruptly and turned around. "I need some time alone," he spat.

He immediately felt bad when he noticed the hurt look flutter in the blink of her lashes, but he turned and kept walking. On the way out, Webb held up his all-access pass and auctioned it to the highest bidder. A rabid fan offered him two hundred dollars. He shoved the cash into his wallet and flagged down a taxi.

CHAPTER FIFTY-TWO · HAMPTON INN, PHILADELPHIA, PENNSYLVANIA

September 7, 2007

Back at the hotel, Webb kicked himself for leaving. He gave up backstage passes and front-row seats to sit in a hotel room and flip between reruns of *Friends* and *Frasier.* The regret multiplied until it was all he could think about. He picked up the phone. Bree answered on the fifth ring.

"We're getting a record deal," Webb blurted, knowing it was intriguing enough to keep her on the line.

"That's great. Congratulations," she said. It was her neutral voice—she wanted to sound supportive, not excited. "How?"

Webb described everything: the studio, the session, the bar, the concert. Bree listened. When he ran out of things to tell her, he asked her to come to Philly.

"I think they're going to offer us a contract tomorrow and… it's crazy. I just wish you were here," he said.

"I have to work tomorrow, and my car is a piece of shit…"

"Yeah, I know," he said with a laugh, picturing her Hyundai rattling down I-80. "But you're invited if you want to come."

He gave her the address to the hotel and his room number but could tell she wasn't writing it down.

"Good luck tomorrow," she said softly. "And when you get home we should hang out."

A surge ran up Webb's spine, radiating through his ribcage until he was sure he was glowing.

"That would be cool. I'll have my people call your people." He cringed at how cheesy he sounded.

"What?"

"Nothing. It was a stupid joke. I'll see you when I get home."

He hung up the phone and fell back into bed.

WEBB HAD been asleep, actually passed out, for hours when the door to their room beeped open. Chris flung himself on the bed, slamming into Webb with the full weight of his body.

"Holy shit, that was awesome. I can't believe you bailed, man. Those guys are so hilarious. We were in the bus. Do you understand that?" Chris shook Webb to punctuate each word. "Inside. Their. Tour. Bus!"

Webb sat up in the bed to escape Chris' body slams. As he slowly crept into consciousness, the regret of storming away set in. The only one he'd punished was himself.

As Chris described the beds, the kitchen, and the couches inside the bus, Webb got angrier at himself, but he kept saying, "That sounds cool," or "Wow," to pretend he was fine with his decision to come back to the room alone and watch TV. *Top Gun* had been playing on HBO in the room when he fell asleep.

"Where's Charlotte's room?" Webb asked.

"Two doors down on the left," Chris said, taking off his shoes.

Webb climbed out of bed. He was sure Charlotte wouldn't keep rubbing in the awesomeness of the night. She opened the door a second after he knocked.

"Can I crash in your room?"

She thought for moment. "As long as you promise not to make fun of my bedtime routine."

"I promise."

He sat on the empty double bed and watched her methodically trail oil along the exposed lines in her scalp. Her movements mesmerized him as she bunched up sections of her wild curls and secured them with satin scrunchies.

"Is this what you do every night?" Webb asked.

"I know my beauty seems effortless, but it takes work to look this good," she joked. "Does it ruin my mystique?"

"No, not at all, it's kind of fascinating."

She secured the last puff in a scrunchie and walked over to him, hands anchored to her hips.

"So are you going to tell me why you punked out tonight?"

"I felt sick," he said.

"I'm calling bullshit on that. Tell me the truth."

"That *is* the truth," he said.

"Something's bothering you. I can tell. Do you want to talk about it?" She sat next to him and placed a hand on his arm.

"I don't know. I feel like I don't have any control over what's happening."

"I know you don't want to sign with Parse, but I think it's your best move. This is it, Webb. You don't get a bunch of chances to make it in this business."

"I don't think that's true. I mean, you said we're really good. And if we're really good, more than one label will notice, right?"

"No! Most of it is who you know and being in the right place at the right time—like when we met."

Webb shook his head. "Don't you think it seems too fast and easy? Shouldn't we have a lawyer or something? I mean, we haven't even played out anywhere real."

"I don't think Parse would object if you want to have an attorney look over things. Do you have one?"

Webb clutched his head in his hands. "No, I don't even know an attorney other than Edgar Snyder."

Charlotte laughed softly. "Parse isn't injuring you in a workplace accident."

"But Edgar doesn't charge a fee unless he gets money for you." Webb played along, repeating the catchphrase from the local attorney's commercial.

"That could work, since you're broke," she said, pulling the covers back on the other double bed. "Can we talk about this tomorrow? I'm exhausted." She sat on the edge of the bed, methodically pulling off her bracelets and rings.

"Yeah, sorry," he said, watching her smooth lotion on her hands and arms. "Do you do this every night?"

"I told you that you couldn't judge my beauty routine if I let you stay here. And since I can't tell you to fuck off, I'm going to have to tell you to shut the fuck up and let me sleep."

He watched her slide under the covers and turn off the light. He lay back in the bed. Eyes open, thinking about the contract, the future, how intensely lonely he felt. He rolled onto his side to face Charlotte.

"Why don't you say 'goodbye'?"

"I told you, it's bad luck for me."

He turned on the light next to his bed. "I know, but why?"

She exhaled slowly. "If I tell you, will you leave me alone and go to sleep?"

He nodded.

"When I was twelve, my parents were going to a party. I was pissed off because they wouldn't let my friend sleep over. They tried to hug me when they were leaving. My mom said that she loved me, and all I said was 'goodbye.' A tractor-trailer lost control on I-80 and came over the divider. That was the last thing I said to them."

Webb swallowed, unsure of what to say. "I'm so sorry," he said finally.

"I promised myself I would only say that word if I never wanted to see someone again. Now, it's a weird OCD thing for me. I know it's stupid."

"I don't think it's stupid. You were just a kid. We all say things like that. I'm sure they weren't mad at you about it."

"But I still have to live with it. Now will you turn off the light and go to sleep?"

Webb thought about Charlotte carrying around the guilt for something that seemed inconsequential when she said it. About things he should have said to Bree. About not taking chances because he was too scared.

"I can't sleep," he said, sitting up. "I feel like doing something that I shouldn't."

"You're not going to shut up, are you?"

He stood and walked to her bed. As he perched on the edge, a look of concern flashed across her face. His throat tried to seize up before the words got out, but he said them too fast.

"No, because I want to kiss you."

Her face softened as she propped her body up. "Then do it."

He hesitated for a second and gently placed his fingers on the curve of her jaw, inching his face toward her. She stopped him.

"Just promise me one thing," she whispered.

"Anything."

"Promise me this won't make things weird."

Webb nodded and pressed his lips to hers. Her skin heated under his fingers. She moved closer. Her lips relaxed into his, suffocating him with the desire to give in to the impulses that could destroy their friendship. He didn't care. The only thing he could think of was how deeply he needed Charlotte now.

Her hands inched up under his shirt, skirting around to his lower back and then up. He pulled the barrier of fabric over his head so his chest was bare. She climbed into his lap. The pressure of her legs, the feel of her tank top against his exposed skin, was almost too much. She tugged on his pants. He slid his hands up her shirt until the tips of his fingers found her breasts. His thumbs ran over her nipples. Her back arched away from him. Trailing his fingers around, he pushed up the length of her spine. He tugged her tank top up and over her head.

"Do you like me, Charlotte?" he asked, kissing along the trace of her collarbone.

"More than I should," she whispered.

Her words created a storm of urgency in him. He flipped her onto her back, pressing his pelvis into hers. His desire growing, pushing against the barrier of his boxers. She wiggled free from her underwear.

His mouth moved in a frenzy across her skin. He couldn't decide where to kiss or touch. She grabbed his hand, directing it down. She guided his fingers until they learned the movement that made her respond with a rush of quick breaths. Her hips jerked, her knees fell away.

She gripped his waist and pushed down until he plunged into her. The torrent built inside him as their bodies moved. The connection of her skin unearthed a desperation in him. They twisted and writhed together until it burst, and they both fell into silence.

CHAPTER FIFTY-THREE - GLEN HOPE, PENNSYLVANIA

October 3, 2007

They had a week to lay down tracks for the album. The tour started in November, which meant they all had to drop out of their senior year of high school to cross the country.

Webb agonized over how to tell his mom. She wasn't one for a lot of rules, but finishing high school was important to her.

"It's a legally binding contract," Webb said. "I signed it, and I'm eighteen."

"I can't believe you didn't talk to me about this. Can't you finish school before you—"

"If you leave this house, you are never welcome here again," his stepdad interrupted.

"Gary!" His mom stepped between them.

"That won't be a problem. I hate this fucking town. I'm not going to get stuck here. I want to do something with my life."

His mom's jaw hardened. "Are you saying that we never did anything with our lives?" she asked, eyes narrow, hurt.

Webb tucked his hands into his pockets but didn't answer.

"When you fall on your face, don't even think about coming back here. You'll have to find somewhere else to crawl back to," his stepdad said.

Webb picked up his bag and headed for the door. "Go fuck yourself, Gary."

Gary's fist reeled back, but Webb ducked out the door before it made contact.

"Go ahead, Webb. Just leave," his mom said and fled up the stairs.

"You're a fucking loser, Webb. Just remember that. You're a fucking loser," Gary yelled after him.

Webb glanced at Bree's house, wishing she would come out to witness his escape, but her door stayed shut. He walked up the road to the Sunoco to wait for Chris.

A WHITE, road-rusted van idled in Chris and Brent's driveway. Parse had said he'd find a tour bus for them, but they had all expected something better. Through the veil of thin paint, Webb could still read the remnants of the van's former life. A large purple cross bisected the words "New Salvation Life Church Choir."

They didn't have a lot of gear, but the van seemed too small to traverse the country.

"Do you think Brent's ego will fit?" Chris asked as they pulled up.

"Being seen in that thing might make it shrink a little," Webb said as he got out of the car. "Will it even make it out of Pennsylvania?"

"Yeah. Why wouldn't it?" Brent asked, loading a duffle bag in the back. Webb shoved his guitar and suitcase into the van and settled into the back seat.

They had to be in Pittsburgh for a show that night, then a few clubs in Ohio, then on to Chicago. By November, they would be somewhere on the West Coast, away from the winter and their families over the holidays.

It bothered Chris and Brent more than Webb. The only person he might miss was Bree. He didn't even get a chance to say goodbye.

Charlotte slid into the back seat next to Webb.

"You're coming?" he asked, surprised.

"I told you, I'm along for the ride," she said.

"She's dropping out of school to go on tour with us. Isn't that badass?" Chris asked.

"Correction: I'm not dropping out. I'm homeschooling."

"You can do that?" Webb asked.

"Yeah, and you can do it with me if you want to graduate," she offered.

"Sure," Webb said.

"You dorks can study while we go out and act like rock stars," Brent snorted.

"Don't you think you should have a backup plan?" Charlotte asked.

"Maybe if we end up on some 'whatever happened to' show, then I'll think about getting my GED or something. That's a big maybe," Brent said.

CHAPTER FIFTY-FOUR - SOUTHSIDE, PITTSBURGH, PENNSYLVANIA

October 3, 2007

B rent insisted on driving all the way. The van struggled up the winding mountain roads on Route 22. There were times when Webb wasn't sure if it was going to make it to the top.

He imagined the engine blowing black smoke all over the road, trapping the five of them inside as they helplessly crashed through the tiny guardrail. He pictured the metal barrier giving up and letting them slip over the edge to their deaths.

Maybe that would be better. An easy way out of the new life that Webb felt unprepared to face. It wasn't that he didn't want to succeed or to live this dream, but there was part of him that liked to picture destroying himself before he had a chance to fail and prove Gary right.

He looked over at Charlotte, who was too focused on her book to notice. He glanced at the cover: *Great Expectations*. Webb turned to the back, where Garrett was sitting alone with his head resting on the window, eyes closed. How was it possible to feel so alone in a van full of people?

When they saw the skyline of the city, even Chris stopped talking. They were playing a real show. Before the tour, they had kicked around a few bars in Altoona and State College; they even played Pizza King in Coalport, but now they were playing a venue that was twice as big as any place they'd played so far. What if no one came?

As they pulled off the highway, Chris started to read the set list that Parse had given them, but his words were muted by the turbulence of the weak window seals and the struggling engine.

"This is the same fucking set list we've played for the last four gigs," Brent interrupted. "You don't need to read it."

"I want to read it. It makes me feel more prepared," Chris said.

"Well, we're not using it, so forget it. We're going to play what I want to play."

"We should listen to Parse," Charlotte said.

"This is my band," Brent snapped. "Parse isn't going to be there. He doesn't control everything we do."

Webb watched Charlotte's eyebrows shoot up. Her eyes squinted into an *I know you didn't just say that* look, but she shook off the confrontation and went back to her book. By the time they pulled up behind the club, the tension had sucked all the air out of the van.

Brent slammed the gearshift into park and said, "Start unloading. I'll get someone to open the door."

Webb almost protested, but he was happy for a break from Brent.

"So now we're his roadies?" Chris grumbled, swinging an amp out of the van.

Garrett silently unloaded a nest of tangled cables while Charlotte grabbed a bag of guitar pedals and said, "Suck it up, fuck nuts."

The back door opened, emitting a puff of stench that smelled like sweet, vinegary beer and sanitized vomit. They filed inside, arms loaded with equipment. Brent stood next to the stage, overseeing the procession.

They piled everything on the stage and went out to get more.

"Damn, that's nasty," Chris said. "Do they ever hose this place out?"

Charlotte, who could usually handle anything, put her sleeve over her nose. "Who would come here?"

"Who cares," Brent said. "If people are drunk enough to hang out here, they'll be drunk enough to love us."

Webb stepped back outside with the alibi of smoking, but he really wanted to get some fresh air. Charlotte came out with him.

"You let it get weird," she said.

"What? Really?"

"You hardly talk to me anymore."

He pulled in a deep breath of smoke, debating how much he should tell her. Her clear, aqua eyes drilled into him, dissecting his thoughts, watching the lies form and evaporate.

"It's not that. I'm nervous, and it smells like the scene in *Stand by Me* where that kid eats the pies and pukes everywhere..."

"It's too soon. I can still smell it in my nostrils," she said.

They stood in silence for a few beats.

"I feel like I fucked up on so many levels," he said finally.

He wasn't sure if he meant with Charlotte or Bree.

She grabbed the cigarette from his mouth and took a drag. As she exhaled, the weight on Webb's chest dissolved. He watched her jagged tooth pop out of the corner of her mouth as she handed the cigarette back to him.

Webb took it, thinking about how it had touched her lips seconds ago. He wanted to kiss her again. He dropped the cigarette and ground it out with his foot. His arms wound around her, pulling her into his chest.

"What are you doing?"

"Making it weird," he said.

She shoved him away so hard, he lost his balance.

"Don't," she said firmly.

"I'm sorry. I didn't mean to—"

"We have to stay friends. You're the only person I like on this tour. Please don't fuck that up for me, Webb."

"I want to make it better," he said. "Give me a good reason not to."

"It will only make it worse. Trust me. Let's erase everything that happened and go back to being friends—for me."

He nodded, surprised that her words didn't hurt as much as they should; he wanted her to be happy.

CHAPTER FIFTY-FIVE - SOMEWHERE IN NEW MEXICO

December 14, 2007

Each stop on the tour was better than the last. By the time they made it to Chicago, they had found a rhythm performing together. When they arrived in Los Angeles, they took a few weeks to record a full album.

The better they got, the more girls followed Brent back to whatever shitty hotel they were in that night. Brent always managed to get his own room, so Webb, Chris, or Garrett took turns sharing a bed.

Webb saved almost everything he made on the tour. He'd fill his pockets at the continental breakfast: bruised fruit, bagels, yogurt.

At night, Webb and Charlotte would hang out, watching TV, and if they happened to be free on a Monday night, they'd watch *How I Met Your Mother*. If there was a basketball court nearby, they would take turns beating each other at Horse.

Some nights, Webb would stay in the room writing new songs. He'd tried to call Bree a few times, but she was always out, probably back together with Jason, doing things seniors in high school did.

By the time they made it to New Mexico, Webb had enough songs for another album. He shared them with Charlotte before the show that night.

"This might be the best song I've ever written," he said.

"What's it called?"

"'The Reasons,' I think," he said and started strumming.

His voice started as a soft mumble at first.

"I can't hear the words."

"You know I can't sing in front of people."

"Just sing the fucking song. Pretend I'm not here."

He closed his eyes and tried to picture that he was alone. His throat tensed, but he pushed through until he was singing at full volume.

When the last chord rang out, she almost jumped off the hotel bed.

"That's an amazing song. Play it again," she said. She pulled out her phone and recorded while he sang it a second time. "That is the song that will make you famous."

"You think so?"

"Um, yeah." She paused for a moment then said, "You know, it's hard for me to understand why you're so hung up on her. She's kind of an asshole."

"That's a dick thing to say."

"It's the truth. I mean, the way you talk about her in your songs pulls my heart out and makes me want to hand it over to you. But she's not a nice person. You're this musical genius, but you're so stupid with everything else."

"I'll pretend that's a compliment," Webb said.

Charlotte looked over to the window. "You're right. It's the best song you've ever written, even if it's about her." She looked back at him, and he saw something different in her eyes. Not her usual determined stare, but a sadness.

He bit his lip, unsure of what to say. The truth was he didn't think about Bree when he wrote anymore. Maybe his songs were on autopilot, or he was simply recycling the same emotions from years ago, but the process of writing "The Reasons" felt different from his first songs. It seemed easier, more hopeful.

The glimpse under Charlotte's guard made Webb want to kiss her again. He set his guitar down and leaned into her, hoping she would meet him halfway. She inched forward toward his lips, and he closed a little more distance between them. Her eyes started to close, and Webb lifted his hand, ready to slip it around the softness of her neck.

"Is this ok?" he asked.

She answered with an "Mmhm."

His lips were almost on hers. "Are you sure? What about making things weird?"

"I don't care about weirdness right now," she said and pushed her lips onto his.

The first sweeps of her tongue inside his mouth rushed down through his whole body. The tickling waves of his nerves rose in his stomach and plunged down, sudden, chaotic, terrifying. He kissed her back with everything he'd kept from her since Philadelphia.

She slid her hand under his shirt. Every stroke of her fingers stunned him and made it harder to pull away. He knew he should stop—for her. But he didn't.

CHAPTER FIFTY-SIX - A CLUB IN COLUMBUS, OHIO

January 27, 2008

"Parse got one of your songs on TV. It's airing tonight," Charlotte shrieked as she hung up the phone. They were setting up for a show in Columbus, the second to last stop on the tour. "I knew he was working on this, but I thought it would be next year."

"And he's just telling us now?" Garrett complained.

"He probably didn't want to say anything until he was sure," Charlotte said, defensive.

"Which one?" Brent asked.

"All he said was it was a shitty teen drama."

"No. Which song?" Brent corrected.

"I've told you everything I know."

Webb's phone rang. It was Bree. He glanced at Charlotte. She was defusing Brent's oncoming rant. Eager to escape, he walked to a quiet corner.

"My mom died," she said as soon as he answered.

"She died? How?"

"She's been sick for a while. She got pneumonia a few weeks ago, and… I thought you'd like to know."

"I'm so sorry, Bree. Do you have a place to stay?"

"Your mom invited me to live at your house until I pass the boards," she said, sounding drained, flat. "After that, I don't know."

"Do you want me to come home?"

"Why would you do that?"

"Your mom died. I don't know. It seems like a big deal..."

"It's fine. I'll be ok. But thanks. How's the tour?"

Webb struggled to continue the conversation as if nothing happened. If that was what Bree needed now, he would do it.

"It's good. We sold all of our CDs. I'm sick of hotel rooms, though. Oh, and they're playing our song on a TV show tonight."

"That girl went with you, didn't she?"

"Charlotte? Yeah, she's here." He swallowed. He wanted to sound casual, but when he said Charlotte's name, his voice rose a little.

"Well, I have to go call family members and stuff."

"Wait," Webb said, trying to think of a way to keep her on the phone. "Did you get the letter I sent?"

"The concert tickets?"

"Yeah. Do you think you can come and see us in Philly?"

"I don't know. I'll see what I can do," she said. "There's a lot going on here right now."

"I miss you," Webb said.

"Good luck at your show," she said and hung up.

THE NEXT day, they were on the top charts for downloads on iTunes, and their CDs were on backorder on Amazon. Their final show at the Trocadero sold out. When they arrived to set up, fans were waiting outside.

Charlotte fielded calls and emails from bloggers and reporters who wanted to interview them. If touring was crazy, this new level was certifiably insane.

"Parse wants to get you in the studio as soon as the tour is over," she said. "He's booking time in New York in February. Can you be ready by then?"

"Yeah, I guess," Webb said. "I have to—"

"We'll be ready," Brent interrupted. "We have a month. That's more than we had for the first album."

Sure, Brent could say that. All he had to do was learn the songs and sing them. Webb was doing all the real work without the notoriety, credit, or groupies.

Not that he wanted them; Brent had to be a walking petri dish of STDs.

"What's the rush?"

"Hans Taff has a last-minute opening. Parse booked him to produce the album. It's the only time he's available for the next year."

This meant nothing to them until Charlotte listed the albums Hans was behind; at least a dozen of the best albums over the last two years.

"It'll be fun," Chris said, patting Webb's back.

The break they so desperately needed from each other wasn't going to happen anytime soon.

"I need to go meditate or join a cult," Webb said and walked back to the green room.

Charlotte knocked before coming in. "Can I interrupt, or are you meditating?"

"I decided on joining a cult instead," he said with an embarrassed smile.

He'd lost his shit in front of her before, but it felt different now.

"Let me know if you need help finding a cult. I'll make sure it's a good one that won't ask you to drink cyanide-laced fruit punch."

She sat gingerly next to him on a brown leather couch that would probably look more white than brown under a black light.

"You're always there for me. It means a lot," he said, moving closer to her.

"I love you," she said. "You're my best friend."

He took her face in his hands and kissed her again, and she didn't stop him.

"This is a terrible idea," she said, kissing him back.

WEBB DIDN'T speak to Brent before they went on. It was better that they didn't talk at all. The opening band came offstage in a blur of excitement.

"That was awesome," the lead singer said, throwing his guitar down on a stand.

"I've never seen this place like this," the drummer said. "We've played here at least a dozen times. This is one of those shows you talk about for years."

"Fucking magical," the bassist agreed.

As soon as Webb ran on stage, he understood. It felt like they were enveloped in the feeling you get on the first sunny day in spring. They thought their shows were packed before, but the energy of a real full house electrified them.

Charlotte stood in the wing of the stage, closest to Webb. His fingers found every perfect note on the neck and a few improvised riffs to fill in. The crowd was still clapping and yelling for more after one encore, but they didn't have enough songs for another. They had to leave them wanting.

Webb ran offstage right to Charlotte and kissed her, pushing his fingers through the braids that she got that morning.

They stayed just offstage, lost in each other until one of the bouncers tapped Webb's back.

"There's some hot chick out there asking for you."

"I'm busy," Webb said, waving him away.

"See? It's already starting," Charlotte said against his lips. "Told you."

"See? I don't care. Told you."

He kissed her harder.

"You look tired. I should get you back to the hotel," he whispered.

She bit at his lip. "But we have to stay to pack up."

"I think Brent can handle it."

Charlotte laughed. They snuck out a back door.

CHAPTER FIFTY-SEVEN - UPMC ALTOONA, ALTOONA, PENNSYLVANIA

January 23, 2016

There were four other families in the waiting room, but only Webb and his mom were there for Bree. He felt like there should be more. He felt like she deserved a waiting room full of people.

His mom settled back in her seat. A selection of gossip magazines was stacked on either side of her. From what Webb could determine: "to read" and "already read."

When he figured out her system, Webb picked up an *Us Weekly* magazine from the "already read" pile, but he put it back down as soon as he saw an article about Brent and a supermodel in Cabo last fall.

He turned to his phone and checked his Twitter feed. News about the show was trending with the hashtag #WheresWebb. He texted Charlotte.

Webb: Hey

Char: Hey. Any news?

Webb: She's still in surgery.

Char: When will you know?

Webb started to type, but he felt weird updating Charlotte on Bree.

Webb: A few hours. Six to eight they said. I think she went in an hour ago.

Char: Returned the car. Glad I got the extra insurance. Do you need anything? Food?

Webb: Not hungry.

Char: I don't believe you. What did you eat today?

Webb thought about food and realized he'd hardly eaten anything.

Webb: A Slim Jim

Char: Swinging by Five Guys. I'll drop it off before I leave.

Webb smiled so big that it caught his mom's attention.

"What's going on over there?" she asked.

"Charlotte's bringing me a burger. Do you want anything from Five Guys?" he asked to draw attention away from the look on his face.

"I'll get something in the cafeteria," his mom said, looking back at her magazine.

When Charlotte texted him that she was outside, Webb went down to meet her. She pulled up in front of the main door and held the bag out the window.

"Don't you want to come in?" he asked.

"This isn't my scene. Besides, I have to do damage control from last night."

Webb walked around to the passenger side and opened the door.

"I hate eating in hospitals. Can I eat in here?"

Before she could say no, he climbed inside. Charlotte steered the car to a parking space.

"Mandy" by Barry Manilow was just loud enough to hear.

"What the fuck are you listening to?" he asked.

She turned the volume all the way down and smoothed the side of her hair. He immediately regretted his tone. He'd never seen her embarrassed.

"Barry Manilow is my guilty pleasure, ok?"

"You always surprise me," he mused. He paused for a beat. "Char, I have to tell you something."

"Don't say anything bad about Barry," she warned.

"I wasn't going to."

"Really? Are you confessing that you secretly love Barry Manilow?" Charlotte teased.

"I'm being serious. This has nothing to do with Barry Manilow." He clenched his jaw. "I haven't been honest with you."

She straightened in her seat. "Don't look so fucking stoic. You're freaking me out."

He'd started it. He wanted to tell her since that night in Philly, but all this time, he was afraid of what would happen once she knew. But he owed it to her. She'd come all this way, organized his life. She deserved to know.

"They're all about you."

"What are you talking about?"

"The songs. Everything after the first album. They're all about you."

Her face steeled, and her eyes narrowed to a degree of anger he'd never memorized. "Why are you telling me this now?"

"I don't know. I had a lot of time to think. I realized that I've based my whole existence on the wrong things."

She covered her face. She whispered, "Get out," through her intertwined fingers.

"What? Why?"

"Get the fuck out of the car, Webb." She turned her head toward the window.

"Charlotte, whatever I did wrong, I didn't mean to."

"I said get the fuck out of the car!" She stomped her feet in the footwell so hard that the Jeep shook.

"No, I'm not leaving until you tell me why you're upset."

"You of all people should know how it feels to love someone that will never really love you back..."

"That's what I'm trying to tell you. I do love you," Webb argued.

"No, you don't, and you're too fucked-up to see that."

"I've loved you since the second time we met. Every song after that has been about you—"

"I know you believe that right now because you're searching for anything to hold on to. But if that was true, you wouldn't be here."

Webb pressed his face into the window, letting the cold glass numb his forehead.

"I'm here out of habit," he said. "But I realized I came here to say goodbye. I love you, Charlotte. *You* are everything to me."

"You jeopardized your entire career to come up here for her, and you're trying to say this is all about me?"

"Yes! Exactly." He smiled. She finally understood.

"You're such an asshole." She looked away from him. "I was going to wait to tell you this until after the tour. I took a job with my uncle's label."

"You what? Why?"

"If I'm going to run my own label in three years, I need to work at one."

"But I can't survive in the band without you."

"You can't survive without someone to pine for, but I won't let it be me."

Silent tears slid down Charlotte's face. Her chin dimpled and trembled. He took it in his hand, sweeping his thumb over her skin.

"What can I do to prove it to you?"

"Make it easy for me. Let me go," she whispered.

"I don't want to do that. I want us to be together."

"And I thought I always wanted you to say that—at any cost—but it's not good enough for me."

She kept her eyes focused out the driver's side window. Webb opened the car door. Before he closed it he said, "Fuck off, Charlotte."

"Goodbye, Webb."

When she drove away, his breath followed the tail lights. He wanted to chase after the Jeep, but he knew there was nothing he could do to make any of it right.

CHAPTER FIFTY-EIGHT - THE HAMPTON INN, PHILADELPHIA, PENNSYLVANIA

January 28, 2008

Charlotte's head rested in the crook of his arm. He traced her profile with his finger. He revelled in the way her naked body felt against his.

"Is it weird yet?" he asked.

Waves of drunken laughter filled the hall outside.

"Sounds like they're back," Charlotte said.

Webb burrowed into her. "I can't deal with them right now. Can I stay here tonight?"

The hotel was sold out. The four of them were supposed to share a room.

"It's a bad idea, but I guess I can make an exception."

Webb concentrated on the smell of coconut oil on her skin, ignoring the fervent banging down the hall.

"I like bad ideas."

"I know you do."

THE NEXT morning, Charlotte poked him awake. "Free breakfast ends in twenty minutes." She was already dressed, her suitcases stacked neatly by the door.

Webb grabbed her leg and pulled her back into bed.

"That gives us ten minutes," he said.

"The muffins will be gone by then, and you'll starve," she teased. "I have to make sure the other assholes are up so we don't miss check-out again."

They stepped over Chris, who was sleeping in the hall.

"What are you doing?" Charlotte asked.

"Brent. Girl," Chris mumbled and pointed at the door.

"Where's Garrett?" Webb asked.

"Lobby. Chair," Chris answered.

Charlotte banged on the door. "What the fuck, Brent?" she yelled.

A few seconds later, the door opened and Bree peeked her head out. Guilt. She'd driven to Philly like he'd asked her to. She had to know he spent the night in Charlotte's room.

"He's still sleeping," Bree said, squinting from the bright light of the hallway.

Then, pain. She was the reason Brent had kicked out Garrett and Chris. He couldn't look at her.

"Tell him we have to check out in an hour," Charlotte said. She grabbed Webb's shirt and started pulling him away. He resisted, wobbling in place, like the floor had turned to liquid beneath his feet.

"What are you doing here?" he asked Bree.

"You told me to come," Bree said. "But you were busy." She cast a scowl at Charlotte.

The last four words hit his chest like a wall of anguish.

"Why didn't you tell me you were coming?"

"I thought I'd surprise you," Bree said.

"So you slept with Brent when you couldn't find me?"

"Why do you care? It's not like you were alone." She folded her arms across her chest.

Charlotte tugged his shirt harder. "Come on, Webb. Let's go downstairs."

Webb stood still, unable to move.

"Close the door," Brent called out.

Webb's anger bubbled up. He pulled away and blew past Bree.

"You fucking asshole," Webb yelled.

Brent sprang from the bed, scrambling for his boxers. He almost didn't get both feet in before Webb shoved him into the desk. The lamp clattered to the floor. Brent tried to tug his boxers to his waist, but Webb was on him again.

Brent stumbled, tripping on the shorts stuck around his calves. Webb's knuckles cracked against Brent's cheek. The pain from the impact shot through his thumb.

Brent jumped up and lunged at Webb, locking his arms around his shoulders. They grappled, knocking beer bottles to the floor. Webb's elbow. Brent's stomach. Brent's forearm. Webb's nose. The thick release of blood dripped into Webb's mouth.

Webb rushed at him again, but Chris grabbed his arms, holding him back before he could throw another punch.

Brent rolled away, pulling his boxers all the way up. "What's wrong with you?"

Webb kicked his feet, trying to break free from Chris' grip. "How could you do this? You know. You fucking know!"

Bree collected her purse and skirt from the floor. "This is weird. I have to go."

"Bree, wait," Webb called after her. He pivoted from Brent. Chris let go, and Webb started to chase after her, but she had already disappeared in the stairwell.

"Let her go, Webb," Charlotte called after him.

Webb fell forward, catching his weight on his thighs. He wanted to collapse in the hall. Charlotte stopped next to him. "I can't," he panted, still out of breath from the fight.

"I care about you," he said. "But…"

"I know," Charlotte said. "It was fun, but I'm not an understudy."

CHAPTER FIFTY-NINE · GLEN HOPE, PENNSYLVANIA

February 17, 2008

 Webb made sure his stepdad was still on the road before he stopped by to see his mom. Since they came back from the tour, Webb had been crashing on Garrett's couch. He couldn't bring himself to go home and face Bree right away.

A full-size pickup occupied the driveway when he pulled up. A bulky guy lumbered down Webb's front steps with a load of boxes in his arms. Webb wandered inside and called for his mom.

"Up here," she said. He followed her voice into his old room.

"What's going on?" he asked. "What are all these boxes?"

"Oh, they're mine," Bree said, breezing in. "I'm moving in with Seth."

"Who's Seth?" Webb asked.

"You met him in the driveway," Bree said, bubbly, happy.

"Yeah, I figured that much…"

Seth returned to grab another armful of Bree's things.

"Seth, this is Webb. Webb, this is my husband, Seth."

"Husband?"

"We got married yesterday."

"Hey, nice to meet you," Seth said and started down the stairs.

Bree grabbed another box and followed Seth out to the car. Webb turned to his mom.

"How long have they been together?"

"I don't know. He came into the salon for a haircut a few weeks ago. I guess it happened fast."

"And you let her marry him?" Webb said in a high whisper.

"It's not my place to tell her what she can do. I'm happy for her. She seems to really like him."

"Really like him? I really like Cinnamon Toast Crunch, but I'm not going to marry it."

"That's a ridiculous comparison, Webster. He has a good job."

"If you ever wonder why I'm not a lifer here, this fucked-up thinking is why."

"Don't talk to me like that."

Webb stood still, absorbing the new reality of his life. Bree had slept with Brent and then married some guy she just met.

"I came to tell you that I'm leaving for New York in a few days. We're recording another album. I think I'm going to look for a place there."

"That sounds like a good opportunity. I heard your song on the radio." She said it the same way she'd say she ran into an acquaintance at the grocery store.

"Yeah, it's a number one song. We're famous. Do you understand that?" He knew he was being condescending, but she was acting like it wasn't a big deal.

"Fame isn't the same thing as success," she said.

"What?"

"I'm just saying that you have a hit song, but it could all disappear in a month."

"Why would I listen to you? You don't know anything about being successful. Look around. The house is falling apart. You can't even pay the electric bill or fill up the oil tank all the way! How many times have we almost been evicted, Mom? That's why Zoe doesn't want to live here.

Not because she wanted to live with Dad. She left because she was fucking embarrassed."

His mom stood and raised her hand. It came down hard on his face. The sting of her palm was cold at first but then grew hot.

"Don't swear at me."

He let the sting blister his cheek, waiting for the silence to break.

"What do you want from me, Webster?"

"I want you to act like my mother." He rubbed his knuckles into his cheek to spread the pain out.

"That's exactly what I'm doing. I'm making it easy for you to say goodbye," his mom said and sat back down to pack another box. Her lip trembled, and she looked away.

Webb lingered behind her for a moment, but she was already pretending he was gone. She wouldn't keep this room for him. This wasn't his home anymore.

CHAPTER SIXTY - BROOKLYN, NEW YORK

February 27, 2008

Webb was the first to arrive at the studio—twenty minutes early. He was still getting used to the subway. A young kid with a shock of white hair crouched over a Nintendo DS in the mixing room. Webb wondered who would bring their kid to a recording session.

"What are you playing?" Webb asked.

"Pokémon Platinum." The kid spat the words out.

"Is it good?" Webb asked.

He threw the console down. "Motherfucker. I almost had it."

Webb backed away, uncomfortable. He didn't know how to act around kids. "Sorry, man. That sucks."

The kid blew a frustrated breath and said, "This game's not even out yet in the US. Do you know how hard it was to get a copy from Japan?"

Webb scratched his neck. "No." He looked around for an adult.

The kid examined Webb and said, "You're early. I like that. What's your name?"

"I'm Webb."

"Hans." He held out his hand. "It's good to meet you. You're a decent lead guitarist, but a better songwriter."

"You're Hans Taff, the producer?" Webb asked, shaking his hand.

"Yeah. Is there a problem?"

"No. I admire your work," Webb said.

"Well, I'm going to ask you to do some weird fucking stuff. Are you good with that?"

"Why wouldn't I be?" Because he looked like he was twelve.

"Some people don't like a sixteen-year-old kid telling them what to do." Hans smiled and said, "Let's get some levels while we're waiting for the rest of the band."

Hans set up a ring of microphones around a folding chair and then walked the perimeter, methodically tapping a few of them into new positions. He sat Webb in the chair, nudging him to adjust his body a fraction of an inch at a time.

"Put this on your head," he said, handing Webb a red beach bucket.

"What does this do?"

Hans flattened his palm on the crown of his own head and pulled his fingers up toward the ceiling. "Resonance. Trust me." He walked back into the control room, leaving Webb feeling awkward and stupid.

They recorded a few seconds, and then Hans told him to remove the bucket. They recorded the same piece again. The bucket went back on. They repeated the process a few more times before Hans invited Webb back to the booth.

Brent, Chris, and Garrett stumbled in while Hans twisted knobs, slid faders, and cut the green waveforms.

"Who's the kid?" Chris whispered to Webb.

"Hans," Webb whispered back, afraid to disturb the process.

"You've got to be kidding me. Is this a joke?" Brent asked. Webb gritted his teeth. Hans turned around.

"Ready to listen?" Hans asked. "This is without my modifications."

The layered notes fell together. Full. Surprising.

"This is pretty good," Brent said. Garrett and Chris nodded.

Hans stopped the track and said, "Now listen to this."

Colonies of sounds swarmed around their heads. Webb couldn't believe how the moments that seemed so random came together in a perfect, beautiful song.

"Holy shit! That's amazing. How did you do that?" Garrett asked.

"Resonance," Webb said.

THE BAND met at the studio early every morning and worked until after eight each night for two weeks. They had access to a catalogue of studio musicians. Violinists, choirs, saxophone players, professional crystal glass players—anything. Hans wanted to add an extra texture to their songs. Webb and Garrett with buckets on their heads. Chris with a piece of metal tied around his chest. Brent refused to wear any of the modifications.

At the end of the second week, they left the studio with nothing else to do until they launched their European tour in a few weeks. As Webb collected his things, Hans approached him.

"You've got at least four hits on this album," Hans said. "But don't go all crazy and buy things you can't afford."

"What do you mean?"

"I've seen too many musicians sell a bunch of albums and then have nothing to show for it in two years. Just be smart. Invest as much as you can. Live off the free stuff."

Webb thought about Bree's words. How she said she'd never be poor. He couldn't believe he was taking advice from a sixteen-year-old, but it made sense.

"I hope we can work together again soon," Webb said.

"I'll never work with Brent again, but if you ever get over your singing issue, give me a call."

Webb took Han's advice and bought a Brooklyn brownstone, renting out most of it and living in the small studio apartment in the basement. He hired a financial planner to invest the windfall in stocks and things he didn't understand.

Charlotte spent the break in Pennsylvania. Webb knew she was avoiding him. New York. Millions of people, and Webb was the most alone he'd ever been. He tried to fill the emptiness by drinking. He couldn't wait to go on tour. Charlotte would have to show up for that.

CHAPTER SIXTY-ONE - UPMC ALTOONA, ALTOONA, PENNSYLVANIA

January 23, 2016

He went back to the waiting room with his mom. She put down her magazine and examined him.

"What's wrong?"

"I really fucked things up, Mom," he said.

"Webster!" she chastised, motioning to the other people in the waiting room.

"Sorry," he whispered, more to the other people than his mom. "I don't know what I'm doing here. I had everything and didn't even see it. And now I've lost the one person who really mattered. Who might actually make me happy."

"You have to decide to be happy with yourself. But what do I know about anything? I can't even fill the oil tank."

Webb reached out and wrapped his arms around her sharp shoulders. "I didn't mean that," he said and rested his head against her like he had when he was four.

She tensed but then placed her hand on his head and patted it.

"And I didn't want to lose you." Her voice trembled.

CHAPTER SIXTY-TWO · LOS ANGELES, CALIFORNIA

July 2, 2014

"After the tour, I think we should take a break," Brent announced after they wrapped the session for their sixth album. "I want to do my own shit."

Webb walked out of the studio with Charlotte. Every part of him wanted to ask, since they were on the brink of destruction, if she would bend her rules after they broke up. Enough time had passed. They were friends again—best friends.

"So, one last tour," Webb hinted.

"For now," she said. "Don't get too excited."

"I feel like this is it."

"You say that every time you get into it with Brent, but the truth is you need him just like you need Bree to write your songs. It's some sick relationship you love to hate."

"I don't need Bree to write songs."

She pursed her lips and unlocked her car. "That's adorable. Fuck off, Webb."

"Wait. Do you want to grab dinner tonight?"

"Can't. I have a date," she said and hopped into her car.

Webb watched Charlotte drive away as the jealousy began to devour him. His phone rang. It was his mom calling for the second time that day. Unless it was a holiday or his birthday, it wasn't like her to call.

"Everything ok?" he asked, watching Charlotte's car grow smaller.

"I don't know how to say this, so I'm just going to say it. Bree's sick."

"Is she going to be all right?"

His heart fell into her long silence. "No," she said finally. "She needs a liver transplant."

The news lodged itself in Webb's throat. He couldn't swallow or breathe.

"I'll pay for whatever she needs," Webb said before she could ask.

His mom let out a relieved breath. "That's not why I called, but thank you."

Webb saved everything he made, but it was all worthless. It couldn't buy Bree what she needed.

CHAPTER SIXTY-THREE - UPMC ALTOONA, ALTOONA, PENNSYLVANIA

January 23, 2016

A doctor entered the room. They all looked up, but only Webb's mom stood. Had it been long enough? Had something gone wrong? Webb rose, taking a place next to his mom.

"She's in recovery. You'll be able to see her in an hour or so." As Webb's mom collapsed with relief, he caught the weight of her small frame in his arms.

CHAPTER SIXTY-FOUR · WEBB'S APARTMENT, LOS ANGELES, CALIFORNIA

July 5, 2014

The door strained against the deadbolt as the pounding grew louder. His cheek slid on the pool of saliva as he turned his head toward the noise.

"Open the door, Webb!"

Webb rolled onto his back, releasing the stench of vomit trapped under his body. He crawled to standing and stumbled to the door. The trip across the room felt like vague snapshots of time. He struggled with the lock for almost a minute before it slid back. Charlotte pushed her way inside.

"Oh my god! It reeks in here." She covered her mouth to protect herself from the smell. She waded through the empty bottles on her way to the windows.

Webb fell onto the couch, exhausted from the expedition to the door.

"Leave me alone," he slurred into the cushion.

"Are you on something? What did you take?" she asked.

Webb grunted. Charlotte searched the trash strewn around for evidence of pills or needles, but she only found empty liquor bottles and half-smoked cigarettes.

She kneeled beside him. "Are you just a drunken mess, or do I need to call an ambulance?"

"I'm fine. Just go."

"I'm not leaving you like this. Come on, get in the shower. It will make you feel better," she said, pulling on his arm.

He snapped it back. "I want to be dirty."

"Well, I don't want to smell you right now."

She dragged him to the bathroom and helped strip off the offensive layers of fabric. He leaned against the wall as the water washed away the last four days. Charlotte stayed in the bathroom with him. Just knowing she was on the other side of the curtain made Webb feel better.

"I thought you were dead," she said.

"I feel dead." He shut off the water and opened the curtain. She was waiting with a towel, her head turned the other way. Webb let out an amused chuckle. She had seen him naked before. She handed him a cup of water and two ibuprofens.

"Since I know you don't have any food, I'm going to run down the street and grab something. Can I trust you to be alone?"

"I'm hung over, not suicidal."

She flinched away from him. "Ok, but please brush your teeth while I'm gone."

Thirty minutes later, Charlotte was back with a stuffed brown takeout bag. She pulled out two containers filled with rich, garlicky broth, foil-wrapped tortillas, and tamales. Just smelling it made Webb feel better. He sat up on the couch and turned so he could see her in the kitchen.

"I almost got mugged for this menudo," she said, searching his cabinets. "Where are your bowls?"

"I don't have any."

"You're the only millionaire I know who lives like a college student," she said, handing him a plastic spoon and the to-go container.

"There's nothing wrong with the way I live," he said, taking a sip of the broth. "I promised myself I'd never be poor. And look at me. I'm not."

She laughed. "I can't believe you don't see the irony in that. Poor people live better than this."

She sat next to him. He watched the last burn of golden light from the sunset flow in through the window and ignite her face. He wanted to touch her.

"So are you going to tell me why you're trying to self-destruct, or do I have to guess?"

Webb put the soup on the coffee table. He pushed his head against the back of the couch and pinched his eyes shut. He didn't want to tell her, but he had to tell someone.

"Bree needs a liver transplant."

Charlotte sat still. He knew she hated to hear her name.

"That's... wow. That's not what I was expecting. I'm sorry."

"You don't have to pretend to be sorry," he said.

"I'm not pretending. I'm sorry for you. I know how you feel about her."

He cradled his head in his hands. "Even after everything she's done, I still can't hate her."

"That's what makes you... you."

The pain slowly left his temples. Maybe it was the soup, or the pills, or Charlotte, but he started to feel human again.

Charlotte pulled her laptop from her bag and started typing. As he watched her book interviews for their upcoming tour, he hummed a melody he'd been working on.

The soft tap of Charlotte's fingers against the keys added an unorthodox percussion. He jumped up and grabbed a guitar to solve what he was missing in the bridge. Webb sang the words along to the chords, adjusting notes until he had it.

"I like that. Is it new?" she asked.

"I've been working on it for the last few weeks," he said, sinking back into the couch with relief. "I couldn't get past the bridge until now."

"Brent is going to love singing that one," Charlotte sighed and looked over at him, but Webb frowned. "What is it?"

"Do you think I have a bad voice?" he asked.

Charlotte scrunched her face up in confusion. "Are you kidding?"

"No, why?"

"Your voice is better than Brent's. You know he's secretly terrified that you'll get over your stage fright, and he'll become obsolete. You're a better guitarist, a better writer, and a better singer."

"I sound like a ten-year-old boy starting puberty when I sing. Bree even—"

"Bree is a sociopath and a narcissist. I'm not even saying that to be mean. I don't know how it's possible, but you have a very skewed perception of her *and* of yourself." Charlotte tucked her feet under her. "I'm glad, though. It's probably the only reason you're still a nice guy."

"*You* have a skewed perception of me," Webb countered.

"True, but when you're not afraid to sing, you have an amazing voice."

He shrugged off her compliment. Even though he knew she would never lie to him, he didn't want to believe her. He changed the subject.

"Who was your date with?"

She focused harder on her typing. "This guy I met at my yoga class."

"For real?"

"Yes, for real," she scowled.

"He can't be normal."

"Actually, he's the most normal guy I've met out here. He's a writer. He's been around the world," she said.

"I'm a writer, and I've been around the world."

"Yes, but he actually went out and saw things. You hide in hotel rooms. Plus, he's not complicated."

"That sounds like a dig."

"I just mean that he's the kind of man who would show up at my house at dawn with a hot coffee and no expectations."

"I don't even know what that's supposed to mean."

"Exactly my point, but I still love you," she said.

CHAPTER SIXTY-FIVE - UPMC ALTOONA, ALTOONA, PENNSYLVANIA

January 23, 2016

Before he could enter the recovery room, he had to wash his hands and wrap a sterile gown over his clothes. Webb hadn't seen her in so long, at first he thought he was in the wrong room.

Bree's eyes were closed. The machines next to her bed stretched their tendrils down to her arms and under her gown. Her heart beeped in green bumps on a screen. He shuffled closer, feeling like he was invading her privacy by being there, but wanting to reach out to her at the same time.

He sat in the chair next to her bed. She stirred, but her eyes stayed shut. After a minute, he collected enough confidence to reach for her hand. Her eyes fluttered and then relaxed. Webb looked down at her arms, yellowed from the toxins and fluorescents. He tried not to look at the puffed-up skin around her elbows.

"Seth?" she whispered, keeping her eyes closed.

He had spent so much time worrying how he would find his way to her and hoping she would still be there when he arrived that he never got to sort out exactly what he would say.

"It's Webb," he whispered back.

"You're supposed to be on tour. What are you doing here?" she mumbled.

"I wanted to tell you that I loved you."

She took a slow breath and let it out. "Please don't say that."

"I wouldn't be who I am without you," Webb said.

It was the truth.

Her lips, cracked with dry, white lines, stretched into a thin smile. She opened her eyes enough to look at him for a moment.

"I hate that you're seeing me like this." Her voice was cloudy, and her words came out slowly.

"I didn't want things to end like they did."

"What do you mean?" She turned her head toward him and opened her eyes all the way.

"After Philadelphia. I didn't want that to be the last time we spoke."

She let out a long sigh. "Have you really been holding on to that all these years?"

"Yeah, I guess so. But I realized it was easy to love you because I never had a chance…" His throat tightened.

He wanted to tell her about the drive, the accident, the memories, but it would end up sounding too sentimental. She blinked to keep her eyes open. He let go of her hand and stood.

"I'm glad you're ok. Goodbye, Bree."

As he started to leave, she called out, "Webb, wait."

He stopped, afraid to look back.

"I'm sorry," she said. "For everything."

He smiled. "Don't be."

CHAPTER SIXTY-SIX - COURTYARD MARRIOTT, PHILADELPHIA

January 24, 2016

Webb balanced a coffee cup in one hand as he knocked on the hotel door. His plane had landed an hour ago. His body was still thick with the grime of two days in the same clothes. The security lock clicked over, and Charlotte peeked into the hall.

"How did you get here?" she asked. "I was on the last flight out of State College."

"I chartered a jet," he said.

She raised her eyebrow. "*You* chartered a jet?"

"Yeah, why?"

"Nothing. It's just surprising." She paused. "What are you doing here, Webb?"

"I've spent the last twelve hours trying to figure out a way to show you that I'm sorry. Looking for some deep wisdom that could erase all the ways I've hurt you and taken you for granted. The only thing I realized is that I don't deserve your forgiveness. But I came to tell you that I love you—just in case you might be willing to forgive me."

Silence. She swung the door back and forth in her hand.

"Do you want to come in?" she asked.

Webb smiled. "I have to get ready for the show, but I wanted to give you this first."

He handed her the cup and then reached into his bag and pulled out a book.

"I'm bringing you coffee at dawn with *Great Expectations*."

"That's not exactly right," she said, reaching for the book. "But thank you."

"I'll see you tonight."

CHAPTER SIXTY-SEVEN - WELLS FARGO CENTER, PHILADELPHIA, PENNSYLVANIA

January 24, 2016

B rent was alone in the green room when Webb arrived at Wells Fargo Center. The name had changed since the first time they were there, but it looked the same inside.

"I didn't think you were coming," Brent said.

"Neither did I."

Webb shifted his weight. He couldn't remember the last time they had talked without a buffer.

Webb cupped his hand over his mouth and wiped off the anxiety of what he had to say. "I've been a huge asshole to you, and I'm sorry. I shouldn't have blamed you for sleeping with Bree. I mean, it was really shitty that you did, but you weren't entirely to blame."

"If it makes a difference, I didn't know who she was. I thought she was a fan."

Webb shrugged. "It doesn't matter anymore."

"I'm glad you came. It's not the same playing without you. Vince is going to be disappointed, though."

"About tonight. I know you don't owe me anything, but would you do something for me?"

CHAPTER SIXTY-EIGHT - WELLS FARGO CENTER, PHILADELPHIA, PENNSYLVANIA

January 24, 2016

They ran out for a second encore. The lights panned across the crowd. Arms extended. Screams. Webb's heart pounded as Brent took the microphone. This seemed like a better idea on the plane.

"Thank you, Philadelphia!" he shouted. "We have one more song for you tonight, but first, I'd like you all to meet someone." He ran offstage and pulled Charlotte in front of the crowd. She resisted, trying to retreat back to the darkness of the wings.

"Philadelphia, this is our manager, Charlotte. Charlotte, this is Philadelphia."

She offered a half-hearted wave and turned to leave. Brent grabbed her arm, holding her there.

"What the fuck are you doing?" she asked through a fake smile.

A road crew member ran out with a stool. Brent motioned for her to sit.

"You don't need this right now," he said, pulling off her headset. Before she could protest, Brent fled the stage, and the stadium went black.

Soft notes broke through the roar of the crowd. Then, a spotlight. Webb walked across the stage and stood in front of the microphone. He watched her anger turn to curiosity, then confusion.

"Even when you say goodbye, I promise not to leave," he sang, looking into her eyes. His voice shook through the first verse. Then something inside him shifted. For the first time, he could hear his own voice. As it came through the earpiece, he didn't hate the sound. He forgot about the crowd. Forgot about the fear. The only thing that mattered was being here with her.

When the last note faded into the applause, Charlotte stood, wiping her cheeks. She leaned into him. "That's the best song you've ever written."

"Even if it's about you?"

She slipped her hands around his jawline, threading her fingers into his hair. Her chin tilted up. He took a moment to absorb the feeling of her palms against his skin. He pressed his lips to hers.

He wondered if she could see every nerve sparking in his body. He imagined his skin growing transparent, showing his blood pumping, his brain celebrating.

"Does that mean you forgive me?" he asked.

She smiled. "Just don't fuck it up this time."

ACKNOWLEDGEMENTS

First and foremost, I would like to thank my husband Adam for giving me a real-life love story. Without his relentless encouragement, I would still be talking about writing a book "someday." Wilbur and Eliza, always.

I also thank my daughter Jules for understanding the basketball games and field trips I missed to create and revise this book. These sacrifices broke my heart, but she never complained.

I'd like to thank my mother for raising me outside the box and showing me thousands of different ways to look at the world. My in-laws, grandparents, and gram-in-law for always supporting me. For GG, who runs the house. Without her, I would have spent more time on laundry and dishes than writing. I appreciate everything.

Big thanks to my beta readers: Mere, Camille, Melanie, Deborah, Carolyn, Laura, and Christine. Special thanks to Camille for reading everything. For helping me "get the wheels on the buggy." I couldn't write a better BFF. I'm so glad your dryer broke.

To Jackie (Ms. Sherman), who only saw the best in me when I was at my worst. Thank you for inspiring me to write.

I owe a huge thanks to Heidi of Blue Moon Publishers for investing in me and this story. My publicist, Talia, for your advice and ideas. The DigiWriting Design Team for the amazing cover. My editor, Allister, for wrangling my comma splices, pointing out my new crutch word, and making sure fucked-up got a hyphen. I also wish to thank the entire team at DigiWriting.

But most of all, thank you for picking up this book in the first place and reading all the way to the end.

ABOUT LESLIE WELCH

Born in Toledo, Ohio, and raised in the North Hills of Pittsburgh, Leslie Welch spent most of her youth concocting elaborate stories. Her high school English teacher encouraged her to turn these creative lies into creative fiction. By some miracle (according to Leslie), her writing skills persuaded Penn State University to accept her. Between her bartending shifts, she studied Fiction Writing and Communications.

Today, Leslie writes at least a thousand words a day on DC Metro orange line trains. Most of them perish behind the delete button. She co-wrote her first book in Harrisburg hotel rooms and diners with her best friend and is now excited to be releasing the first book with her name independently on the cover.

When she's not off exploring the world (or getting caught in irons on Roanoke Sound), Leslie lives in a house full of laughter outside of Washington, D.C., with her soul mate, two cats, two dogs, two fish, and a teenager.

Connect with Leslie:
www.lesliewelch.com
facebook.com/lesliewelchauthor/
https://twitter.com/Leslie_Welch
www.lesliewelchwrites.tumblr.com/
goodreads.com/user/show/32399008-leslie-welch

BOOK CLUB GUIDE

1. Webb doesn't like Merilee but dates her anyway. Have you dated someone you didn't really like? Why?

2. Jason and Webb are best friends in elementary school but grow apart in high school. Why do you think they grew apart? Did you have similar friendships that dissolved once you became a teenager?

3. Bree's actions seem erratic and impulsive. Have you known someone like Bree? Why do you think she acts this way?

4. How did you feel when Webb asked Charlotte, "Do you like me?" (the same question Bree asked him) before they had sex?

5. On the surface, Charlotte and Bree seem like complete opposites. Are they similar in any way?

6. Both Bree and Charlotte suffered from traumatic events in their childhood. How do they deal with these events differently?

7. Charlotte is strong in all areas of her life except one: Webb. Have you ever loved someone and sacrificed your strength to be close to them?

8. Charlotte calls Webb out on his frugal lifestyle. Why do you think he lives this way?

9. Webb's mom and Bree grow very close. Why is this relationship so important to both of them?

10. How do you feel about Charlotte's reaction when Webb tells her the songs are about her? What would you have done?

11. At the concert, Webb finally sings on stage. Do you think Charlotte forgives him too soon? Should she have held her ground?

12. Were you glad that Webb didn't end up with Bree?

WRITE FOR US

We love discovering new voices and welcome submissions. Please read the following carefully before preparing your work for submission to us. Our publishing house does accept unsolicited manuscripts but we want to receive a proposal first and if interested we will solicit the manuscript.

We are looking for solid writing—present an idea with originality and we will be very interested in reading your work.

As you can appreciate, we give each proposal careful consideration so it can take up to six weeks for us to respond, depending on the amount of proposals we have received. If it takes longer to hear back, your proposal could still be under consideration and may simply have been given to a second editor for their opinion. We can't publish all books sent to us but each book is given consideration based on its individual merits along with a set of criteria we use when considering proposals for publication.

THANK YOU FOR READING THE GOODBYES

BlueMⴃon
PUBLISHERS

www.ingramcontent.com/pod-product-compliance
Lightning Source LLC
Chambersburg PA
CBHW060639260626
47161CB00008B/2921